Elijah Rising

Published by inGroup Press, a division of inGroup Marketing, LLC.

Book cover photography by Laura Kate Berkowitz. Book cover layout by Shelly Rabuse (http://www.rabusedesign.com).

inGroup Press and the inGroup Press logo are trademarks of inGroup Marketing, LLC. The inGroup Press logo was designed by Shelly Rabuse.(http://www.rabusedesign.com).

First published 2011

ISBN-13: 978-1935725084

Visit our website: www.inGroupPress.com

Elijah Rising

Lyn LeJeune

inGroup Press

Chicago, IL

Our youth are desperados.

—Warner Fabian

BLACK PROPHET ON A FIERY CROSS

Put it over the plate for Jesus.
—Billy Sunday

Elijah Rising

The frigid winds of February have assaulted New York like the beginning of an ice age. Then I saw him. I had given up on him, believed he had been blown away with the winds of time. I'd been afraid that he had perished, sucked into the meanness of humanity in these last years. But today I stared at his picture; there he was majestic before me, his words no longer hued in bright colors just for me, but in plain and simple black and white, spread out on the table like demented symbols. Black hands held and threw the words at will.

Little Washington is standing upright on a platform, the sun is streaming down on his shoulders, his eyes are frenzied. He is wearing a suit and tie. In his outstretched hands he holds a Bible, as though he were making a final offering to the world: Take this or you shall be left behind. Is that what he is saying to the crowd? The caption below the picture reads: *Young Negro preacher speaks in tongues. Elijah Broom captivates even white southerners in Tennessee revival.* An alien hand rubbed my back, leaving bloody nail marks as it moved from my neck to my spine. That was the pain of it, the shock. Little Washington, now the great Elijah, had made his way to a home, a place to belong, and planted himself into the mind of America. Did he respond to a calling, one that had been with us as we looked down upon his dead mother that long ago day? Had God spoken to him from his open Bible, reached out and clutched his soul in big, white fabricated hands? The portent of this intention, this transformation, was captured in the picture. Elijah was out for retribution. The article goes on to describe him: *He is not five feet tall, a little yellow Negro that speaks about the flood and redemption. When asked if he is going back to Africa with Mr. Garvey, he says: 'No sir, I am in the presence of the divine country. I have followed the instructions of my Lord, for I have been called to cleanse this land. Alleluia'. And then he kisses his Bible. He always kisses his Bible.*

My hand reached for my eggs and bagel, but they had become like pieces of my past, inedible. The smell of salty fish that I had come to love in these last years had turned to carrion of days past, putrid, stale, deadly. I walked back and forth from one end of my flat to the other for hours. I was flushed, my skin prickled, my head was airy. Was this really *him*? How could I be sure? I looked at the picture over and over again. It was like he'd been suspended in mid-air, a jumping man, hand held up to God,

2

the Bible elevated, as though he was telling God, *you, you read this*! *See what you have done!*

When I sat down again, I forced myself to finish reading the article, because I knew it was without doubt my Little Washington. No longer the Little Washington of the streets. I was captive to his form. I could hear him: *His screeching is unearthly, it fills the tents with something either heinous or holy; it infects the people, no matter their race or their standing in life. Dogs howl to dear heaven when he begins and ends.* It was as though I had entered a petrified forest, alone, but summoned forward.

I had once imagined him dangling from a tree branch, his head askew, neck pulverized from the constant swinging. He would not die. That image bombarded me far too many times and I remembered every moment in the last few years since I'd touched him. As it always was and will be, the voices joined me. They laughed at my intentions. I had no choice, in my heart, but to go to him. I believed that he needed me. *A fool hath no delight in understanding, but that his heart may discover itself.* That I mumbled and babbled as though it were my personal worn proverb, biblical in scope, true or false to the world. I did not know which. *Think Michael*, whispered the voice, *is it true or is it false?*

As I packed my bags, I knew that I was going into a dangerous place with my body and my words. I had turned this thing with Washington–no, I shall call him Elijah—over and over in my mind thousands of times. What place had I in his life? What was he to me and America? Did I need him to go on with his preaching? How extraordinary that they would allow his preaching, this black man, in this age of fury. It is January, 1921, and the world still reels from the death of millions in a war that served no purpose. Was *Elijah* real to them? Had they forsaken their own sins to let him speak? He—a black child, no a black man— saying that *He has spoken to Him?* Believable? Or just some sideshow freak fit for Ringlingtown. Elijah was the first person who had truly softened my heart, whose life had brought tears to my eyes. He had changed my life, was the rod that sparked me to move or die. How could I not go to him?

America, here is your Black Prophet on the Fiery Cross!

Elijah Rising

The train ticket I'd purchased with a light feeling brought me to Memphis, Tennessee. I had to make my way across this land, where Elijah Broom was to give his next revival. It took three weeks. I had never been out of New York; never out of the city and its rush of life. I felt as though I were headed for a distant planet where the air would be sucked from my lungs and I would live a life in suspension. Oh, how I had longed for that.

As the train moved, jerked, braked and strained forward (it was difficult to write!), I tilted my head and scanned the buildings. The ironworks that covered the tracks were like lace on a hard woman's dress. I think now only about the thrill of that hunt. I saw words tumble from my hand as my eyes devoured the new country into which I had been born but had yet to discover. On my lap was *The World,* opened to several articles I had recently cut out and stuffed in my coat pocket. I remember that Elijah loved baseball and, because he could not see the great games, he probably had imagined the sport in mythic proportions. I understood that, at long last. A new stadium for the New York American League Club will be ready for the 1922 season. How would Elijah like to see baseball in the Bronx? Would he think that baseball is like preaching? Would he understand it as a thing of beauty no different from the Holy Scriptures? The other article was about the new statistics on lynchings in America. Oh, what a devious country we live in; baseball, lynchings, and God all in the same thought. I also brought two presents for

Elijah: a recording of a new song called "Listen to the Mocking Bird" and a box of Belle Mead Sweets. If he does not have a recording device, I will get one. I wisely brought along a supply of my own chocolate slabs. I cannot survive without two things: chocolate and rye.

When I thought of him, he came over me like a whisper, like palm fronds brushing over my arms, seraphic and cool, a breath that speaks of salvation and souls and sinners. This is young Elijah Broom, swept away, swept away. I swallowed his image like the chocolate that I treasure, the thought of him lifting me up from my melancholy hole. It all melts on my tongue. What purpose is laid before us on this earth? Is this what we call destiny? Is it the end of a long ride on an iron horse that I am drawn into, completely, irrevocably, as though the end of my life will be nothing but hurting pleasure?

The train was leaving the city. Chug, chugging like the whispering of a child. Excitement filled my chest so that I was about to burst. I was a child at last, adventure before me, for I journeyed to a new America, where I would learn a new language, a way of speaking straight to mind, heart and soul!

My sleeping car was mahogany and green like the forests of this country. The window was a glass that was opaque with the hue of blue steel. I had before me on this long and wondrous journey my own moving picture show. It flashed and flickered and stopped so that I saw America before me. But there was no sound, no voices, except those that battered me from inside my head. The screams from across the ocean and over the plains reached me in my pursuit of Elijah, who calls himself "Archangel." I thought that, in the end, he was being too presumptuous to succeed in this calcified world.

The porter who attended me as we left the bursting metropolis was so white that he seemed translucent. Blue veins snaked from his chin to the corner of his eyes; eyes that were blue like mine, with reddened sclera. His nose was wide and crooked and purple. He wore a white jacket that was tucked at the waist and the gold letters on his right breast announced his rank. He is not union, but he was my servant. I did not hand him the two cases that held my journal, rye, candy, and books. I handed him my clothes cases and he probably stored them in the belly of this beast that I will ride over this land. I imagined riding a great and garish dragon, snaking over mountains, through lakes and across rivers, breathing fire, warning those who would stand in its way. My bags contained my worldly possessions, the ones that would not give me much pause should they be lost or stolen or simply given to a poor sot who needed such ugly clothes. I no longer cared about such loss. Who needs such things to ride the American dragon?

I settled back in the soft observation car chair and wished only for smokes and chocolate. My stash of rye was in my Pullman. I was so bloody amazed that I was on this great train, that I was headed out to a new land, to an adventure, to a soul that I knew, without doubt, called to me. And I was in awe of how far I had come in less than four years. I had grown into a strong man. I smiled often, even when I couldn't see the surface cause. It was a peace that had grown from within me, that had always been there, I think. What I longed for was before me: The future. I had to find faith, a way of bringing all parts of me together, a way of becoming whole and indivisible. Imagine it, not to be shattered by passing words and jibs from those you love and do not love so much or at all. That is what we all aim for, isn't it? That's the mystery of each life. Deny it all if you will, but we all come back to looking straight into that mirror. But first, we must walk through the door.

Luck. Is there such a thing in this world or are we the masters of our journey? Lucky that *The Dial* took up my idea of writing an exposé on religion in the fundamentalist South. All I knew of it was Billy Sunday and now the face of Little Washington, Elijah, and of course, what I had read. But reading is not the experience. I laughed at my assignment: *Go and write a report on that old time religion. You know, William Jennings and pals. Yeah, that Negro kid. Good idea. And don't forget, you're going to be right smack dab in the middle of the passionate mob. The Klan and sharecroppers can be dangerous for a Yankee. Don't get yourself hung.*

It took almost three weeks to get to Memphis. I saw rivers and bridges and mountains and fields of growing life. I crossed this land in the spring, the blooming time. New York to Philadelphia, Baltimore, Washington, Richmond, Lynchburg (How in the hell had the town gotten such an odious name?), then Roanoke, Bluefield, Knoxville, Chattanooga, Decator, and finally, Memphis. Names that were as American as Sinclair Lewis and *Main Street*, yet imported from England and even the ancients. Like Memphis, where once the Nubian peoples owned the open sky. What is Memphis in America? I wanted to hear the rush of water as the train sped across the rivers. I wanted the force, loud and unending, the wind massaging my face so that tears gathered in my eyes and washed away the smoke of my past. I loved the whistling porter, waited for the piercing sound that was like an arrow in my heart. Pierce my solitude with the sound of a black man's breath!

What brought me the greatest satisfaction was that I had left Mother and her dreadful life behind: A life of privilege and ignorance. But to pass the time when darkness overtook the train I decided to write her a letter. I finally had the nerve to tell her what I was, how I had changed and did not need her anymore:

> *My Dear Mother, no, Dear Mother, no, Mother: I am headed into the Promised Land, leaving a life that offered me complete and utter uniformity, opportunity for nothing but what was. This land is so great, so vast, that a man can*

simply vanish, leaving no clues. I reread Fitzgerald's This Side of Paradise last night as this train (does it really belong to Father?) rumbled south. It is a story of people whose lives are dismal and of their own making. Empty Mother. And I said to myself, by God, what if this is all true, this life that Father paints; worse, that our days will not get any better, any different, even when we walk to this side of paradise. Read the book, Mother, and you may have one, clear inkling about my journey. I think that I dwell too much on my childhood. But it is the only way that I can accept that I have lost a great deal of the play of it all. The joy! Isn't childhood supposed to be joyful? You asked me to forgive you, and I do. Always, Mother, I forgive you and the times and the constraints of your sex and position. You are so wealthy, yet I can now write that you and your crowd are poor in spirit.

And then I added this line and then erased it, coward that I still was: *I love someone.*

The train moved on and I was as hungry as a bear. I was afraid that the food would be of little consequence to me, dull and tasteless. My senses had been screaming for something, screaming in my head as always at sundown. So that one evening I thought that I would go out of my mind. I fumbled my way to the dinning car. It was exquisite and I settled in the first class seating. The waiters were dressed completely in white, and their gold buttons caught the rays from the flashes of low sunbeams. If it had not been for the awful black bow ties they wore, I would have been at peace. I detest bow ties. The waiters were so attentive that they flipped open the starched napkin (the sound hurt my head) and laid it across my lap. I looked down and saw that it was monogrammed with the initials *H* and *H*. Father's railroad. But I was anonymous. Then I was served. Then I went out of my mind: honey, rice, cold duckling, cheese, strawberries, peaches, cinnamon, sugar and cream. Then my smokes. All this while I watched the sun retire beyond the darkening horizon, moving with deliberate haste into sparkling clouds that turned from orange to red and then soft purple and finally black night. I should have felt desolate, lonely; but I did not. I knew what hope was. I knew what it was to be nothing but

7

a man of contradictions, completely filled with lies I told only to myself. I couldn't wait to tell them to Elijah.

The *Times*—or whatever newspaper that was available when we made a stop—was delivered to me personally. I mostly did not remember one newspaper from another. There was a report of the flight of Jack Knight. Yes, flight! A man in an airplane traversed the country, from Nebraska to Chicago. Behold the first transcontinental delivery of mail! We were rushing back and forth across this land by all means. What does the future hold? How fast can I get from here to there? How does being in one place faster than before change the course of the world? How will we perceive the future when we can get from there to there in four hours rather than three days?

Another day, another newspaper: Two days ago Warren Gamaliel Harding became President. I could not see that he was capable of bringing much to the country. He promised to make life in this country normal again. But really, could he sustain the swank and sway that got him elected? And at sixty percent?

One morning the train was held for hours; a reprieve from the constant rocking that was beginning to put my stomach on the bum. From my window, I watched black men loading bananas onto trucks, their hats suspended on the back of their heads like magic. The porter (his name was Jim) told me that they were called reefers. The other men, with custom hats and hard collars, were the inspectors. *What are they inspecting?* I asked. *They looking for poisonous spiders*, he replied. I shuddered, of course, and

Jim laughed, assuring me that the creatures could not make their way into the Pullman cars. *Ya can sleep well, Mista* he said. I looked up at Jim and at his dark eyes, the white sclera with a tint of yellow.

Do you know about this preacher? The man called Elijah Broom.

Yes sir, he smiled. *Gonna bring his children out of the Promised Land. Sure thing. My mame she seen him preach. She tol' me it was like seeing Jesus in a black skin. But we know better, don't we mista?*

I nodded and smiled back at him and said: *That remains to be seen.*

A week along and the train was heading down a mountain, screeching and rumbling and rocking. We were moving into a benighted country. Will there be sucrose, water, rest, and peace? I think not. There will be no more buildings of the metropolis, but a great inviting world

8

pushed to the horizon. I felt it, a great sucking wind pulling the train as though the steam and coal and steel and iron were but illusions of power. Nature trumps. Rocks sprouted along the tracks, growing higher and more preeminent with each measured mile. Energy pounded the earth and then I saw great mountains puncture heaven. Blue-shaded hands of sky wiped the face of the mountains and gray mist rose, unclothing the jutting crests. It was America primeval.

If I was on a Baldwin train, I will one day inform Father that it did not give such a smooth ride. The last two days had brought my stomach to a boiling point. I had been able to nibble on my chocolate, but little else, despite Jim's insistence that he bring my meals to my cabin. The train had burped and stalled so that my stomach had lost its contents once too often. It seemed we ran headlong into a great storm. Finally, the rocking stopped.

I almost went crazy because of too much movement and sounds. I thought I had left my ghosts behind in my flat, in New York, there to haunt someone else. But last evening they came back, laughing and taunting me, vowing that they would follow me for the rest of my life. I wanted to make peace with my demons. Again and forever. Because my journey became bloated with colors and pounding noises, the voices of the people on the train had turned to babble. The train became a sideways tower that was crushing me. I could not wait to end this journey. The excitement had vanished.

Were it not for the kind Jim, who attended me and did not condemn or laugh, I swear to God I would have jumped from the speeding train.

Finally, the rocking stopped. We made it. Weeks had gone by. When I asked about Elijah at the station and then the hotel, I was told that he had already moved on.

I was sick and my sickness rumbled in my head and all I remembered was arriving in a red room. Gold shimmered around my head and a big lady put her hand on my cheeks. When I finally came back to the world, I had discovered that I was in a brothel in the dingiest digs of Memphis. I had been there since the train arrived, carried on the cart that Jim borrowed from the engine master. How kind of him to want to save a white man in this godforsaken world.

Elijah had preached and moved on to a town miles and miles from here. I knew this because Pearl, the head prostitute (oh, she is so very soft

Elijah Rising

and human) went to his tent meeting. She told me that Reverend(!!) Broom is all the rage and her girls found such hope in his admonitions. Hope and admonitions seems contrary.

The fever left me and I was served a new treat that is meat covered with a thick red sauce and burned on an outside fire by the cook at Pearl's. Good old Jim saved my cases, so my chocolate and rye softened my moods so that I could explore Memphis before moving on to find Elijah.

The morning was warm and I went to a store called the *Piggly Wiggly*. That was new experience for me. Rows of food and factory-made items lined shelves. Free black women were wandering about and buying goods. I stocked up on smokes and candy, dried meat, and ink for my pens and a pile of paper. I was a little afraid that I would run out of my writing tools and that would be the end of my career, my will to move on in my life. I had to send something to *The* Dial. What a discovery on my second day in Memphis! There was a new music that pulsated through the city, maybe even all of America. I thought it was sad, but then again joyful and hopeful. Contrariness again! It was called the Blues. The music was like a wave up and down Beale Street here in Memphis. They told me a man called W.C. Handy was here. I had not seen him yet, but what a great article he would make for *The Dial.* Yet it all reminded me of Elijah, and I needed to get going and find him. I made notes on "The Blues: A New American Sound" and finished the article before bed.

I said my good-byes to Pearl and the ladies. I'd had enough fun poked at me for not using their services.

I traveled by wagon heading to Elijah's tents. I sat on old newspapers and pulled one out to read as I waited for a broken wheel to be repaired. Had God really sent Elijah? In June, the white citizens of Tulsa burned the Negro area called Greenwood Flat to the ground. The pictures were horrendous: A young man stretched out on a wagon, just like the one I rode to find Elijah, on display like a prize from a gruesome hunt. The Mississippi flowed near the road on which I traveled. My geography was weak, but I felt I had to go there to see if the raging waters had picked up the bodies that had been dumped in the rivers outside of Tulsa. I got my answer, and I still to this day don't know whether I was up to the sight.

Bodies, all belly down, passing by me as I watched from the banks as though great Rome had fallen and any hope of civilization and the rule of law had vanished.

Is one river of death connected to all others? Can bodies travel from New Orleans to Canada through the vista of America letting the onlookers know what has happened? Perhaps, I thought, as I smelled the rot of flesh; we had become numb already, in this new century.

I turned away from the scene and walked along a road that was black and desolate. It reminded me of photographs of the Western Front, with the bodies of young men supine and lifeless, gone, gone, millions of them gone, washing down the rivers of Europe and everyone too exhausted, too spent to gather them up.

And I was standing in Tulsa, standing on the western edge of America, and I was thinking that yes, one river of death is connected to all others.

I saw Elijah in the gloom of September light. He had been a silhouette against the New York sky when I had first laid eyes on him. That day he was that again, but greater, stronger, like a sword perforating my heart. I wrote what I saw quickly so that I could get it down just right. This instant in time, I thought, would give me courage to approach him. I took two steps forward and asked myself: Will he remember me?

Have you ever felt your entire body pinch? That was what happened when I watched Elijah wash himself outside his little tent. Spindly arms still, but muscular and rippling now. His head was thrust upward and against an alabaster cloud that had moved over the sun. He was beautiful, like a beatitude of my granite Catholic years.

Elijah, I whispered, *you are the force of what love is.*

And he turned to me and smiled, as though he had known that I was coming. *Well, Michael, my man, at last. You still have the gift of turning an instant in time into a portentous event. I can use a man like you.*

There is nothing like autumn in Tennessee. The dried cornstalks rustle through the night air and bring peace. And the whispers are cunning, because they tell me of battles between good and evil. I was with Elijah

11

and he knew me right off when I walked to him. He had held out his hand to me. *Welcome friend.* Nothing else was needed for me to become a man of God.

I stayed in a small tent near Elijah's. His tent was in back of the main encampment. Elijah was not the main preacher in this road show of God. Hiram Bell was the head of the moving church. I wanted to tell Elijah: You are being used, a sideshow to draw the crowds, the little Negro preacher, a second act, a second banana. I had seen the night before how the people laughed when Elijah came on stage. And all I could think of was convincing him to soon strike out on his own.

The first night I worked on my first report to *The Dial.* I told Elijah what I was doing and he simply said: God's will is that I be known. And this is what I wrote:

> *Every morning, just as the sun moves from behind the low hanging blue mountains, I watch this man who calls himself Elijah, The Prophet, Archangel, emerge from his small tent. It is the beginning of a new time for him, one that tests his body and spirit. He faces the sun, bows, then kneels. He covers his face with his right hand. It is too large for his small body. In his left hand he holds his Bible. After what seems like an eternity, he begins to read. I cannot hear the words, but no matter. I feel them like arrows through my heart. What kind of miracle is this?*

I was waiting for Elijah's first preaching gig. Winter was the color of decay. Our quarters were at the end of a long line of tents. The line began with Preacher Bell's tent, which, unlike all the others, was large and warm and that was where food supplies were stored. Mrs. Bell was obviously disdainful of Elijah. I had heard her call our row of little tents the *nigger shanties* and huffed that she couldn't understand why God had sent Elijah, *the potent prince of darkies*, to her husband. Then she'd shake her head and spit on the ground.

The night had finally come. It was Christmas Eve. That morning I watched Elijah as he read his morning breviary. I had heard that Bell was going to leave for Texas soon, that he'd decided that he'd had enough use

12

of his black prophet. The tone of the rumors made me afraid that Elijah's life, and the lives of his compatriots, and my life, were all in danger.

The celebration began. It was full of fire-cooked cornbread and a large roasting pig and old corn that had been hidden by the young children that followed Elijah. They were the orphaned of this land. Twenty tenters stayed with Elijah. I made twenty-one. The night was full of cold and heat. We sat around the campfire on rocks that never warmed, even with our bodies perched like baby birds waiting for worms. A small girl named Liza sat on my lap. She was big-eyed and emaciated. I gave her a piece of chocolate. Elijah gave her a black rag doll. Elijah was dressed in a black suit with a starched white shirt. His head stuck out like a purple lollipop and the fire made shadows dance around his face. He raised his hand and said that he had written a special verse for the occasion, one that Jesus had whispered in his ear that very morning. We waited until the time came. And then he ran up to the stage, smiling. I closed my eyes and drowned in his voice.

> Come unto me, says Jesus
> Say I
> Oh, yea, all you heavy laden
> With sin
> Come unto me, says Jesus
> Say I
> Oh, yea, all you world-weary.
>
> Come unto me, says Jesus,
> Say I
> Oh, yea, all you hungry to be born
> Again
> Be healed, be healed.
>
> Redemption, redemption, is
> All there is
> Redeeming power,
> Jesus
> Redeeming power of the angel
> Me.

Elijah Rising

I went to sleep with the sound of Elijah's voice and the voices of many others that had traveled with me on my journey to Tennessee. I was afraid. I went to Elijah and he was sitting, staring at the fire and drinking a cup of what smelled like whiskey. I told him about the voices and asked him to please make them stop. He held his hand over my head and laughed, his laughter was rough and penetrating. He said:

You see how I am doing this? Take note for your articles.
You are hearing the voice of God's angel and that should
put you at peace. Yes, Michael, even in death the voice of
an angel will put you to rest.

I truly did feel better; the voices raced away. And I thought that Elijah would always compose the continuity of my happiness. And then he moved away from me, folded his hands between his legs and smiled. *There, you see,* he said, *you can fool lots of the people lots of the time.*

GO DOWN

The Spirit of the Lord came upon Gideon, and he blew a trumpet.
—Judges, 6. 34

Elijah Rising

My name is Washington, just Washington. But you can call me Elijah Broom; that is who I am to the outside world, a man of God, preacher *par excellence*, soon to be Hollywood moving picture star. You must know from the outset, and if you heard my preaching, that only one thing matters to me—the Living God. I am his vessel.

I love America because America has hurt me, tried to take away not only my soul but my entire life. Threw me in the gutter. You, you readers had a hand in shredding my Mama and sister and brothers. Don't even ask about Pap, it's useless; I remember nothing. Let me tell you about brother. The last time I saw him he was hanging from an oak tree, a crude and dirty rope tied around his neck. I think I was four years old. I watched the whole thing. I heard the men standing around the tree scream *higha', pull 'im high', make dat nigger swing.* I was hiding behind a blackberry bush that was full and the berries were big and fat and sweet. I ate them as I watched. And then it was over and his neck broke and then they left him there. I never told anyone that story, especially not Mama. But every morning I'd go back to the berry bush and eat until my stomach hurt and I'd wait for brother to wake up and come and help me pick breakfast for the rest of us. I can't rightly recall how many days I sat cross-legged or how long; I know I waited until the sun came up over the horizon and bathed brother in a godly light and that was when I decided that God had taken him and it was up to me to tell the world about it.

Go down Moses, yelled our preacher at the little church that was sorry and had been burned twice already. *Go down*, and all of us would yell back, *go down*. Until one day I realized that going down was just another way of giving up, letting the white man and America beat us down. Slavery is slavery, I tell you.

Mama took us away up north so we could have a better life, so she could get a job and so could sister. Mama never talked about brother again. We packed up our clothes and a pot or two and spoons and headed out one morning before dawn. There was no business to finish up; we had no business in the first place. Those were the times. If you had nothing, you didn't have to feel sorry about it.

I was happy; happy that it was July and it was hot because I did not have shoes. My feet had already become like leather from all the years, five by then, walking around in all kinds of weather and places. One time I got a bad infection from a cut on my foot and got fever and dry and almost

16

died. But Mama prayed over me and sister cried and gave me lots of water from the river and I was cured. Just like that.

Keep you alls back straight, said Mama. She carried a gunnysack on her back and the pots and spoons clanked as she swayed. Mama was short and thin, like a little gray bird. *Keep 'em pine tree tight so dat whens we gets to the factories da mens can see you alls fine and young to work.*

Poor Mama. She still believed in something. Still believed in that old Bible she made me carry. Her once and never again employer, a Mr. Bob Benoit, gave her that book as a Christmas present. Lord God in heaven, you would have thought he'd given her life back, or at least a ham and turkey. I didn't understand what the big deal was until she sat me down next to her on our only bed, coaxing sister and brother to listen. I don't think they did, because I'm going to tell about them soon. Well, I already told you about brother, so there's no need to repeat that part of the tale. Anyway, I listened. I surely did and the world opened up to me, God spoke and the moon shined down on us like an invitation to a miracle. I knew what my life would be about. And I knew I had to accept the next few years for what they would be and then take the hand of God when he decided to put it out to me. He would come in many forms.

Mama read night after night. *The Lord went before them by day in a pillar of a cloud, to lead them the way; and by night in a pillar of fire.* Night after night she'd read from Exodus, as though she was spinning a spell. *The Lord went before them by day in a pillar of a cloud.*

One day we were walking down a dirt road, the air was cool and clean. Trees that had turned to many colors lined the road. It was beautiful. *Looka, Mama*, I squealed. *God be callin' us.* The wind picked up and I caught three falling leaves; a red one, a yellow one, and an orange one. I spread them out like I was holding a deck of cards. *Look*, I said, turning to sister, *Deys leaves*, said sister. And she wiped her eyes that had become swollen with some kind of infection. By the time we got to the factories, to New York, she was blind.

The clouds ruffled up and a cold wind blew from the north and we continued on. On the second month of our trip, when we had no more food and drank from the streams along the way, a wagon full of little black heads headed toward us and I yelled. *See dera, Mama, it be a chariot of da Lord.*

And you know what? It was.

Elijah Rising

There came a man from Canaan and he drove two large mules toward the setting sun. He wore a hat of pure white that covered his face and we could not see him right off. The chariot stopped and the man nodded to Mama and held out his hand and she held hers out to him and he pulled her into the wagon. So we all hopped in, sitting backwards as the man clucked his tongue and off we went. I said: *Mama she got the gift. She knowed we be picked up.*

The man from Canaan stopped beside the road when night came. We rested by a fast running stream where the water was cold but clean. And we had cornbread and roasted chicken legs. The man he took his hat off so he could start the fire and drink a tin of coffee. His skin was like leather, his deep blue eyes fixed me in a stare and scared me until I shook. He licked his lips and a sneaky smile just appeared like magic on his face. He put his hat back on and it was then that I noticed the little golden emblem at the edge of the bill.

Mama she took out her Bible like she always did. Turned the pages until she stopped and put her hand on the right hand side of the book and squinted her eyes and read.

> *Behold, the days come, saith the LORD, that the plowman*
> *shall overtake the reaper, and the treader of grapes him*
> *that*
> *soweth seed; and the mountains shall drop sweet wine, and*
> *all*
> *the hills shall melt.*
> *And I will bring again the captivity of my people of*
> *Israel, and they shall build the waste cities, and inhabit*
> *them; and they shall plant vineyards, and drink the wine of*
> *them; they shall also make gardens, and eat the fruit of*
> *them.*
> *And I will plant them upon their land, and they shall no*
> *more be pulled up out of their land which I have given*
> *them,*
> *saith the LORD thy God.*

Lyn LeJeune

If I'd had a chance to say my own made up prayer I would have asked the LORD to strike this man for he wore the seventh seal and we were in very big trouble.

They swooped down on us from behind trees and bushes; I think there must have been ten or twelve of them. There were the men who shredded my family, took what was good and hung it up a high, high tree. They tied all of us up. On the hill the full moon made a mighty tree and great shadow, its branches reaching right and left and up. I watched, knowing that these kinds of devils lynched men but rarely little boys and women. Not that they had such a tender part of their hearts, but because it was more amusing. Mama she just kept on screaming that they were Satan come to earth; and the more she screamed the more they laughed. I heard sister sniffle, for as young as I was then, I knew what she feared most. She would have rather been hanged.

I will not describe the lynching of the man whose name I did not know. You have all seen it too many times before, in newsreels, in pictures. Enough is enough. Just remember that I was no more than seven, that my mother wept and my sister went crazy.

When it was all over and I had to live the rest of my life with the image of that man just hanging there limp like an old dead crow. They threw him on the wagon and we again headed north where as the days passed it became colder and colder until the snow fell like feathers from heaven and covered us as we lay in the back of the wagon. Yes, poor sister had got most of the men riled up and they'd had their way with her before we left. I think Mama fainted and stayed that way for days. I watched her chest go up and down, so I knew she wasn't dead. Sister just whimpered like a dying dog.

So there we were, three sojourners who had to live out our lives more broken than when we had started our journey to the promised land. None of the men had touched me, so I lay whole on the blanket and then one night someone threw another blanket over me. I was happy, because then I could watch the sky and the sides of the world through the slats in the wagon, and we moved on. Someone gave me a piece of meat and a piece of stale bread. But, then, there were many times in my life when I had no urge to criticize what was given me. This is what I learned in the weeks before we got to New York and we were dumped in the San Juan slums: *All that you have to do is survive. After that, it's all easy going.*

19

Elijah Rising

Mama worked cleaning the house of a nice man named Finkelstein, I ran around stealing whatever I could get my hands on, and sister disappeared to the street corners selling herself for ten cents with no dancing. Would you believe me if I said that I was happy? I was. I was free. Mama was too busy to tell me go here or there. Sister had become a shade and she would never be a Lazarus. So I lived, and I picked up newspapers and stole books and pens and listened to conversations and learned to read and write. Okay, I know that the hand of the Lord guided me. So what, I had summoned him while holding my Mama's old Bible, told him that he had forsaken us all and that he owed me.

And then one day I found my tickets. Michael Man and Billy Sunday, standing on the street corner watching boys march off to war. And behold before me was a great Tabernacle and the people amassed in front of the little white man who swung his arm so hard I thought it would jet into the sky. *Put one over the plate for Jesus*, he yelled. *I tell you it is Kaiser Bill against Woodrow, Germany against America, Hell against Heaven.* He waved a paper in the air and announced that he had just created, yes *created,* The William A. Sunday Evangelistic Committee of New York City. God had sent me an omen. I could learn so much from Billy: how to captivate a crowd, how to say just the right words, how to summon the Lord at needed moments, how to jump and sway and swagger. I went to see Billy every day until he left to extend his crusade into the hinterland. I was not ready to join him; besides I knew I could do this, have my very own preaching concern.

The most interesting part of that morning was the man I saw watching Billy and taking notes on a pad of paper. Then he suddenly put his pad and pen in his jacket pocket and turned left and entered a building where there was a sandwich board that read: "Recruiting Station." I waited, and then the young man came out, his head bent forward as though he had lost the rest of his life. He rambled away and I followed him as he went from one alley to another looking for something. Looking, always looking. Finally he sat on an old wooden barrel, his hands on his knees, and cried like a baby. There he was, my second ace in the hole.

This is the most important lesson I learned from Billy Sunday: Watch each person, stop at the one you know is the most needy, the one who you know had lived empty days, had yet to find something to live for, was as lonely as an old mule in the back forty. Set your mind on that guy

20

and pull him in. Tell him that Jesus loves him and that he will never be alone again. Offer him all the things he most wants. Hang back at first and do not scare him. Once you have him and you know that all he wants to do is throw his arms around you forever, take him, make him yours. He will follow you into the fires of hell. And that is how you put another one over the plate for Jesus.

So I waited until I saw him coming down the alley on a late morning. I jumped out, did a little jig and looked slyly so that I knew he had seen me, then I took off. I did that for many mornings until the day I saw him come with a big white box. He had brought me a present, so this was the day of our meeting. I hung back and he approached me and I just let him have me.

He asked questions and I answered him as though I were some poor old nigger kid lost in the slums. I ate the cake, or at least part of it, and told him I would bring the rest to my sick Mama. I did not tell him about brother; there are some things in life that must remain unsaid. But I said sister was out selling her body, because where I lived, that's just what sisters do. He listened with this surprised look on his face, like he didn't know what went on in his own town. The richer grow richer and stupider. He dropped words like war and poverty and a man named John Reed. I didn't know or care what he was talking about. I just needed him, pure and simple. The Lord had sent him to me and in the days or years to come, he would be my left hand of God. You know, the expendable one.

This Michael he wanted to see where I lived. So I cried and led him to the cellar where Mama had died a few days before. He offered to bury her for me once he realized she was dead. I read from Mama's Bible and he listened and made a promise to take care of her body. He gave me a wad of money. He left, then I left and headed for the Tabernacle, ready to find out where Billy had gone and to follow him. With Mama gone, I was ready.

I had made another important friend while in New York. A social worker named Angie. She was like an angel, really. A kind person. Her black hair was always scattered here and around like a thousand springs. I wanted to say good-bye and perhaps get a sack of food. She told me to stay put because there was panic in New York. *Panic?* I asked. How could things get any worse? *There's diphtheria and scarlet fever and tuberculosis*, she said. *Well*, I snickered, *I best be out of here. Stay hera*

Elijah Rising

and I be dead come morning. You will disappear in the fog of time, she said, as though she were reading a poem. *Dat be da point,* I said, and ran down the street before she found out about Mama and hauled me to an orphanage.

I never resented the Lord for making me little. It served me well. I hopped on trains and wagons, hitchhiked, all the while following Billy's path, the schedule that had been printed in the newspaper. Everyday I'd unfold the article, read it over, ask whoever was around what day it was and how long to get to a place called Memphis. Two months and five days after saying adios to New York, I was in Memphis, squirreled in a cellar with a bunch of other black boys. I was miserable, my teeth had turned almost black and my gums bled every time I took a bite of old carrot. One day a man with black hair and penetrating eyes arrived at the cellar with two fat white women. The other boys scurried out as fast as rats, but I stayed because, you see, I still believed that the Lord was guiding me and here sent another angel of sorts. *My name is Hiram Bell,* he said, patting me on the head. *Come with me, we are out to save our daily allotted ones who are sick and lost to God.* I wanted to say, well, mista, ya done found a man who found the Lord way before you did. But I kept quiet and went with one of the fat ladies as she hugged me to her as though I'd forgotten how to walk. We went to his tents and a doctor examined me and wrote something on a yellow piece of paper which I later found out was some kind of medicine that made me sicker than a dog.

But, all in all, Hiram Bell was a decent man. He was tall and gaunt and I thought he looked a little like Abraham Lincoln. He had the exact needed effect for a preacher man. His wife could have scared the life out of Satan. But I was in Bell's hands, I was his mission, and he taught me everything he knew about preaching to the crowd. One night he let me preach. *Practice,* he said. *There's lots of Negroes need saving.* I practiced and I was good, even the white crowd clapped when I jumped and yelled for the Lord to land in the house of the weary. A drought had descended on the land and the farm crops dried in the fields. The people were hungry and tired, the winds blew in from the Great Plains all the way into Memphis. So I offered what they needed. *The Lord will vanish the locusts from the lands, we will have rain, and all things will become green again.* On and on I went. And they yelled and clapped and Bell told me that I was pretty good at preaching.

One night a newspaper man came to the meeting and took my picture.

I knew he would come. One morning I knelt praying and reading from Mama's Bible, trying to get the words that would be sufficient for the evening preaching. Bell gave me ten minutes. He would preach for two hours.

Now the LORD said to Abram, "Go from your country and your kindred and your father's house to the land that I will show you. I will make of you a great nation, and I will bless you, and make your name great, so that you will be a blessing. I will bless those who bless you, and the one who curses you I will curse; and in you all the families of the earth shall be blessed." So Abram went, as the LORD had told him; and Lot went with him. Abram was seventy-five years old when he departed from Haran. Abram took his wife Sarai and his brother's son Lot, and all the possessions that they had gathered, and the persons whom they had acquired in Haran; and they set forth to go to the land of Canaan. When they had come to the land of Canaan, Abram passed through the land to the place at Shechem, to the oak of Moreh. At that time the Canaanites were in the land. Then the LORD appeared to Abram, and said, "To your offspring I will give this land." So he built there an altar to the LORD, who had appeared to him. From there he moved on to the hill country on the east of Bethel, and pitched his tent, with Bethel on the west and Ai on the east; and there he built an altar to the LORD and invoked the name of the LORD. And Abram journeyed on by stages toward the Negeb.

Michael man stood there as though he had seen me just yesterday. He smiled and I smiled back and I made it all seem as though I had eaten cake just that morning. *Well, Michael man*, I said, *I haven't had chocolate cake for some time now.*

FAMILY AND ALIENS

I have seen the silence
Filled with vivid noiseless boys
—e.e. cummings

Elijah Rising

It all began in April of 1917. I waited for war. The world had gone mad. All that was left was for Mr. Wilson to pull the trigger. The debates continued in Congress. But it was all just formality. America had been moving to the edge of the abyss since before the conflict began on European soil. What did anyone expect? Father and his friends needed to feed the war machine, and few if any had the courage or means to stop them. I had heard the discussions for months, facile conversations that mocked the sinking of our ships by U-boats as the deciding factor.

This was my proof: Yesterday, I walked down Park Avenue, measuring my steps like a man who had finally recognized the world for what it was. It was a bleak Saturday, despite the coming of spring, the vanishing chill one expects this time of year. It should have been a season for happy poetry, but the words in verse dripped with dread. Heroes existed for death and nothing more. I stopped at the corner of 34th Street, at the 71st Regiment Armory, where young men were gathering, declaring themselves ready for a war that had not yet been proclaimed. I walked by slowly, trying not to let myself look too anxious. I suppose I was afraid they would grab me. I said good morning to the soldier on duty. Really, I wanted to yell at him: *Haven't you read the reports about the Western Front? Don't you know what a trench is? Do you know what all this holds for you?* But I did not say a thing. I studied his face, knowing that I had to remember him, remember his blue eyes staring up into the night. Then I imagined him calling for his love a minute before he died; it was as though I had been pushed into a waking dream. Already he was dressed for war; muted brown woolen coat to his knees, a long knife belted to his waist, and a gun on his shoulder, the bayonet flashing in the sun. The day was sullen and warm, and I wondered how he lived inside that uniform.

I walked back to Mother's house and tried to understand how a nation can really prepare for war. In spirit, I mean. Do we really expect the slaughter to end just because we march forward with the rest of the armies of the world? I'd heard that a conscript was coming. If I am called, what shall I do? I am almost twenty-one and I'll have to go. And I think of my life and about bravery. Is this a time for heroes, for Ivanhoes, for men taken from a book that we all hid under our beds, entranced by the adventure, taken by the wonder of the spirit that we willingly took deeply into our souls and acted out in play? Yes, I still remembered the charges put to those knights . . . *to trust for their protection, during the dangers of the times, to their own inoffensive conduct, and to the laws of the land.* We spend our lives in dreams and expectations. Those days were gone, my friend.

The word on the street is that the pacifists plan to converge on Washington, to try and convince our government against a declaration. Even Booth Tarkington was to be there. I read some of the materials from the Emergency Peace Federation and I was interested. But this peace was a dream, they must have known that. My God, hadn't they seen those loyalty pledges that already flew through the air? The newspapers were full of them. The newspapers did their part to push war forward, not by inches, but miles. Take an inch and twenty die; take a foot and fifty die; take a mile and thousands die.

I opened the door to my mother's house. I had lived in this house all of my life and still felt alien. It was afternoon and I was alone except for the servants. From the sun porch I could hear their rustling footsteps, faint then louder, as they moved past the entrance to my solitude. The sun porch was my favorite place, where I could see the massive gardens, a replica of the one Mother had seen on one of her trips to England. Along the white brick walkway the daffodils swayed, the hyacinths still pushed a wondrous fragrance into the air. Within a month, all kinds of flowers would bloom, and each month thereafter a succession of colors, all coordinated, would enliven the view from the window. This garden was measured, controlled, exacting, and unnatural. But I took pleasure in the hues of blue and yellow and pink. I should have felt safe there, but I didn't. How can something so beautiful be a hell on earth for me?

Hilda told me that Mother was at a tea given in honor of a new bishop for the diocese. She had given up on my attending church again. I stopped going before I went off to Princeton, because every time I kneeled in an intended act of contrition my sins were repeated over and over again, whether they were real or made up. I laughed remembering the many times, as a young boy, I stayed up at night making up imagined sins for the confessional. Those were the sins that bore through me like a drill, making my bones rent and porous. When I thought of those nights my muscles tensed, I stretched, and I felt that old familiar pain. Doctor Mallon had told me that I was suffering from neuralgia and recommended Sloan's liniment. I prefer Chopin and rye. Mother said that I drank too much, but she still told the servants to keep a stock in the cabinet. Well, for some things I was grateful.

So I cut out the loyalty oath from the newspaper and placed it on the piano while I played. *Will you stand by your country if war comes?* It asked. Who are these people who make up the American Committee on War Finance? And then I read further, listened to the tones and tinkles in my head: *Rich and poor must be ready to make patriotic sacrifices.* But the poor man will make the greatest sacrifice. He will do most of the fighting; because he forms the bulk of the population. He will offer his country more than life itself. If he is killed or disabled, he will leave his wife and children helpless, dependent on charity or the state. I played for a few more minutes and the thought of those words stopped me dead. The arrogance! So the poor were more likely to die because they were poor? They had put wooden guns in their hands already, to practice war, at Princeton and City College. Where do the poor practice war? The aroma of the hyacinths was so strong I could taste it. What does war smell like?

Again I drank too much. I was on my fourth glass of rye when Mother returned. I couldn't bear her harping about the war, her sudden support of the common man. Did she see them as fodder for the cannons and therein lies her support? Oh, Mother, you are so loyal to your class! She had not said one kind word about Wilson, but she was all for war. Mother hated the Democrats!

I escaped to my rooms for the evening so I could avoid her opinions.

The die was cast and we were at war. A vote of 373 to 50 in the House of Representatives. The politicians asked for one million men and . . . three billion dollars! Those figures had been called *respectful* by the papers; the estimations were praised as a step toward giving the war in Europe a quick end. Laugh if you must.

Oh, shit. Now Mother was making war an event. She asked me when I intended to sign up. *Sign up?* I choked. And I knew my voice betrayed me; there I was a boy standing before her again, refusing my role in her world. *Oh, Michael, do be sensible,* she said. *What, Mother, do you want me dead? No,* she said, *I wish you to do your duty.* Then she told me

28

that I would be assured officer status or whatever was necessary so that I would not have to fight. *Oh,* I said, *then I will be the one who directs those who die?* She ignored me and then said that she was going to give a party Sunday, a party to celebrate war. Satan, I think, lived in that house.

The pacifists went to Washington and were assaulted as they spoke against the war, their hands raised, supplicating and empty of weapons, except for the words they yelled at whoever would listen. Sure, the pen is mightier than the sword. Now they were downtown New York and so I rushed to the meeting. I watched them being pushed this way and that, like little children bullied in the schoolyard. One woman said she would not see her sons die, not for something she did not understand. Then a man in a blue suit knocked her down. She fell on her knees. I could not make out his face, but I could feel his hate as he swung his fist up and down upon the back of that pitiable woman. I wanted to help her, but as I looked around I knew I could not; the odds were ten to one. So, that was me: I watched and took notes and I remained far from the crazy crowd.

As I walked along the avenues I heard the clamorous, joyous calls. I saw young men at the colleges standing in line to buy their war uniforms so they could look like patriots when they picked up their girls. If they were not yet bound for the ships that would take them to their fates, they would at least look the part. Only $16.00 for a uniform, issued from Gimbles. The war sold already. I knew many in my crowd will be pleased. Stocks rose, the price of coal was precious.

Late the next morning I put on my cutaway to go out. I was not in a good mood, certainly less inclined toward killing since I finished reading Mr. Beck's new book *The War and Humanity.* It was second-rate mongering. I am not a pacifist, but God in heaven, had the screw turned all the way? My stomach began to twist and I felt a new burning in my chest. At least I had enough smokes to carry me through. The air was warm and noisy. I said this out loud: *Spring is a strange time for war.* An old man turned and gave me a twisted smile, as though he knew the whole story yet to be.

What I saw in the headlines scared the shit out of me. The men at Princeton continued to prance. They were practicing marching through the

29

campus, with bow ties and caps and bare heads. Even baseball players were being instructed in military formation. Batter up!

I couldn't take it anymore, so I went home just as the sun moved below the Woolworth Building. It was a monstrosity. The gargoyles glinted and—should I press my imagination—I could see their yellow eyes smiling over New York's horizon. Was that the architect's intent? The devil may be in the city as well as in the house in which I lived. I thought, not suddenly, but . . . well, I conjured the idea that had lurked in the back of my mind for a long time. It emerged when I told myself that I had to break away, make my own way, before Mother smothered me with her life. So I decided to make a plan while she was at a reception for the Women's Defense League.

The war party began: They came in gray tailored frocks with braided edges and striped trousers and wearing soft hats, oxfords in deep black leather that shined. That was the war uniform of the upper class. And the women wore the new *crepe de chine;* I think that was the name of that soft and flowing material. They were all pink and lime and yellow. But their collars were stiff and bone boiled white and as their heads turned for speech, for laughter, for attention, the blackened curls that adorned every cheek quivered like worms to the flesh. I can write this down simply because that was what they jabbered about: Satin trimmed with *soutache*, braided or beaded embroidery. High-heeled shoes, smiling red, red lips. I welcomed my friend Charles and his girl Helen and her friends Martha and William. The names of youth inflated the air and reminded me of their coming out, their introductions to a society that was then hell bent on their destruction. They were my group, my friends. We grew up in a world that promised and promised and forgave us forever our trespasses. No more! I wanted to shout to them: *Do you not see that it is all different, that we have evolved into bent creatures*? Mr. Darwin: He was before his time.

I hung back, observed and smoked so many Ricoros that the tobacco hurt my stomach and my throat became raw. Champagne was the antidote I used that night.

Mother had purchased a new phonograph just for the "glorious occasion." A new Edison. Mother saw her sanctioned events as always "glorious." She really drove me nuts. The music was whiny and modern and cut at my soul. *da-da-da-di.. Michael, this is your party. These young people are your people. Dance.* I was not an idiot. Mother was a true Calvinist, though she professed Catholicism. She did nothing if it did not bring her success. Practical results was her motto. So what did she get out of this, this war celebration? Oh, I know: Her own self-importance. She actually believed that what she did would in some way change the course of the world. Well, I wanted to tell her*: Mother, one day you will kill someone with your shenanigans.*

I couldn't stand it any longer, and so I slipped away while Mother was not looking. The outside world, the city called to me . . . come, come and see what I am!

What is the relationship between the gospel and war?

I was just too curious to resist. There was Billy Sunday's Tabernacle I had heard about. A monument to the gospel on 168th Street. It was a low building with spires that pointed to heaven. How else could I have described it? It surely had no architectural relation to the great cathedrals. So what did God want from us?

And there amongst the flock, like Jesus at the water, Billy Sunday was entertaining a crowd. He was a small man, with a face like a kind uncle, rugged and smiling, always smiling. And he moved one leg in front of the other, bending forward, drawing his right arm back and threw . . . nothing at the crowd. His hand was empty. Then he hurled that same hand upward, his face turned toward the heavens, and he yelled: *Put one in there for Jesus.* The people poured fists of money into baskets. Billy called his followers God's grenadiers, a name most apropos for the times. Once a sportsman, Billy now pitched the gospel right in there, just like a baseball heading for the soul; a home run. An all around athlete in God's house. This was his afternoon question for the crowd: *Have you the Holy Ghost in your heart?* Well, Mr. Rockefeller was there, and Governor Whitman, Billy between them, all in silk hats. The Tabernacle was consecrated by

31

the powers of government. What more can earthly beings ask for? Billy was out of uniform.

And surrounding this new House of God were recruiting stations, one right across the street so that Billy could, well, just pitch them over. From God to war, a double header. What then was the relationship between God and War?

Was I a pacifist? Even the Quakers, I was told, backed the war. I suppose we all had to cross the Rubicon together.

Home again, home again. I should have known that the great financiers would follow each other to the meat. Father showed up this morning without warning and threw the entire household into a great tizzy. Amelia was a true servant and bowed to Father like he was royalty. I suppose she was devoted to him, and I was surprised she did not leave when he did and go with him to his other house. Why she stayed with Mother is beyond me. She immediately ran to the kitchens and instructed poor Hilda to make Father his favorite sweet rolls and Bolivian coffee, and the other servants fussed and curtsied and just made a general to do. I knew he paid them well. Top dollar, as he said.

Father was his usual frigid self. He turned down his nose at me, probably because I performed no worthwhile duties for him. What had he expected from an only son? To follow in his stead like a wounded dog? How could I have possibly competed with this imposing man? He towered above me, always had, and I suspected that he always would. So I bowed to him and asked him how his health was faring. *Quite up and up, Michael*, he said. I knew his language, the tones of it, the moves, the compression of the soul. *Shall you return to your classes any time soon*, he asked me. *Yes,* I replied. *You cannot manage a fortune until you complete your studies*, he sniffed.

When I was away from him, when courage came to me, this was what I wished for: To be an ordinary man, to throw my hat in the air and feel joy, to lick my fingers after eating, to wear a cap and not a hat, to use the word swell and mean it, or hug a friend in full sight of the world and feel no shame.

Father wanted Mother to go in with him so that he could buy stock in the National Ship Building Company of Seattle. *How much do you want*? she asked him. He told her that the offering was one hundred thousand shares with twenty million available. Oh yes, I understood it all;

those were the times of ships and steel and billowing smoke stacks and tall buildings glimmering in the sun. The city planners were proposing more underground byways throughout New York for us to live like rats. Father got all, but Mother played her hand well so that her surrender was only conditional. To think, this was the way my family waged war.

My stomach was hurting so I went to my room. The hell of it, the doctors said, was my smoking and the rye whiskey that aggravated the situation. Hilda had forced me to take *Man-a-ce* and it had helped in alleviating the pain for a while. At least I could stretch in bed at night and read. *The Red Badge of Courage* and *The Titan* were near my bed, waiting. I had completed the last poems of Rupert Brooke. He haunted me. What would he have been had the war not taken him? Now women were writing war poetry and it was romantic rubbish. It inspired young men to die. *I love you, so go and fight and die.* Is a memory more heroic than the person?

April 17, 1917 and it was my birthday, twenty-one years old, so I decided to get the whole thing over with. Bite the old bullet, raise the flag. I offered myself to my country before I was officially scripted. Well, to hell with it now.

Mr. Wilson made his official announcement yesterday. He called it his "Proclamation to the American People." *The supreme test of the nation has come. We must all speak, act, and serve together!* So I went, despite my rumbling about war. I suppose I simply did not want to be left out of something big.

I left the house at eight o'clock and tramped through the streets until I came to the recruiting area across from Billy Sunday's place. The Tabernacle was deserted. What was I hoping for going there? Divine guidance? I had taken a morning bath, as though cleanliness would be the measure of going to war. The walk did refresh me, or at least it calmed my nerves. I had gotten down to two Chesterfields by the time I arrived. I couldn't take the trolley anyway, since there is an electric car strike going on. The empty green cars passed me by. The clanging sent me into a near rage, as the noise echoed inside my head. I wanted to run into the street, yelling stop it, stop it, damn it all! The thought that Father must be beside himself made me smile. As for me, I'm all for the unions, really, so good luck to the New York Railway Company.

I was prodded and weighed and measured. *I'm sorry, son,* the sergeant said. He looked like a bulldog. *Sorry? Why sorry?* I asked. *You're too small. You don't weigh enough and you checked that you have stomach ailments. Besides, young man, take care of those feet of yours. What feet?* I asked. *You have flat feet*! Then he handed me an official looking form, stamped with these words: ***Classed incompetent to perform the highest duty of citizenship***.

I walked I don't know how many blocks, not knowing or caring where I was headed. I felt such loneliness, such utter desolation. I bought more smokes and stopped at a bar. I had never been in such a place. I remember it had an unusual name like McCauty's or Maloones. I got lost in the voices and smells of easy companionship, got tanked, and somehow made it back to the house.

It seemed I'd slept forever. I woke with a pain in my bowels that sent me reeling and off my bed. I swore to never drink again. Hilda had sent Harold for Doctor Mallon. He looked at me and shook his head and said that I was a disgrace to my family. I got so angry. *Who are you to judge me?* I yelled. *Sir,* cried Hilda, *you'll get yourself sick to dying.* She threw her arms around me and I felt suddenly as if I was a little child again. It had always been Hilda who had held me on those all too frequent days when I had no school chums, or when Sister Blanchette had scolded me for not completing my lessons, or when the world mocked the sublime solitude of my childhood.

I drank so much *Man-a-ce* that I felt that I would die from it, that it was this substance and not blood that was now coursing through my veins. Hands coddled my chin and pressed my mouth to open. No more, I shouted to shadows that had gathered, promising to haunt me through the rest of my days.

I woke the next day just as the sun was setting over the great buildings of the city. The horizon was orange, streaked by a violet tongue that licked at the sky. The sight of New York refreshed me, gave me hope that settled into my heart. I thought that perhaps after it would be all said and done, this great war, humanity would continue on. How could man build such esteemed buildings, create such great works of art, make music that changed a soul from sour to sweet and not, in the end, have courage to go on? Never had I felt redeemed, so ready to participate in the flush of life.

The sky changed from orange to pink to then deep blue as I stood at my window, the heavy drapes pulled back so that I could get as full a view of my new world as possible. Azaleas and daisies had blossomed across the street, and I had not noticed before. I lifted the window and accepted the evening breeze as it touched my cheeks, and the smell of New York was like life. The noise from the tooting cars and the clanging of the electric rails sent shivers down my back. I had awakened from drunkenness to life, from shame to decision, from sickness to action. I had much to do. To make something of myself.

I let the drapes fall back over the window and switched on the electric lamp. Like a kaleidoscope from my childhood, the colors of blue and azure and yellow and green and lavender reflected the light. I had slumbered in the cool grass, looked skyward and waited for the sun to scorch the glass pebbles. It made a world of difference to be right there at that time of my life. The sadness that I felt was for all mankind, and mostly for those who had already perished in the fires of war, for the mothers and children who saw every night the lamps go out in Europe. I was so lucky to stand there, in a great country, where I could just flick my wrist and light was forever mine. Yes, how lucky I had been!

To strike out on my own, I needed a job. So I spent the morning looking through the Man Wanted lists in the newspapers. What was I suited to do? Young man wanted as an accountant, an engineer, a person who sells clothes, a laborer, a gravedigger, stockman . . . the list went on and on. With the war coming and the conscription more and more likely every day, the list would be endless. But I saw nothing that I was fit for. What had three years at Princeton studying business and the classics prepared me for? Gravediggers were what was needed; workers to rid the world of the war dead. I told myself to stop being so damned morbid. Before I had time to get dressed and venture out into the working world, the telephone rang.

I drove to Montclair for luncheon at an old acquaintance's house. He had rung me to tell me that he had received a commission in the army.

Elijah Rising

Charles was a good guy and had befriended me at Princeton, even in the days when it seemed my body had been tossed from one group of young men to another and I did not have the constitution to fit squarely with any of them. He was one of the most intelligent man I knew there and I can say that he was truthful and honest. I would miss him.

The ride was pleasant and I felt as though I were groping for a freedom that lay just beyond my outstretched hand. I had learned to drive the new Velie Mother had purchased. It was designed for seven people and here I was touring through the streets alone and over the bridge that linked one New York world to another. I cruised hatless and glanced at the tumbling water below me and the glaring April sky above.

And I thought about Constantinople and other faraway places that stood ancient and beckoning. Could I make a story of my life that would rival the thousand and one?

The Wesley house rested on a hill, protected by a gray fence and swaying green poplars. Black windowed eyes stared at me, unblinking like shrouds. As I approached upward to the drive, I could see the crowded lawns and colored strings of lanterns stretching tautly from one tree to another. Dance music was playing the harsh rhythms of our times, tunes for haunted, ageless women. I parked the car at the end of a long black caravan. The morning was warm and I could feel a thread of sweat move down my back. I wanted to take off my jacket. The young women were dressed in glamorous purple and silver and gold, not the same old dull pastels of vanished Easters. They had mixes and matches and pulled over hats that hid the sides of their faces. And veils, all kinds of veils, some with imprinted flowers, some with snaking lines that reminded me of spiders. I thought this trend ugly. Why would they want to cover their beauty? I was told not very long ago by a young woman who'd had her fill of whiskey, her thinning and languid body draped over a couch at a seemingly elegant affair, that she wished to be alluring. *Don't men like alluring women*? she had asked me. I told her that I didn't know about other men, but I did not.

The talk was clamorous and high pitched and was all about fashion and war and pity for the families of the dead and pride for the dead themselves. One could know the dead then by names and often by photographs in the dailies. It had become the thing for the newspapers to record the names of Americans killed and wounded in war-related

36

incidents. There commenced among our startled youth a guessing game as to who knew the name of the first American killed in Europe. The whole thing was shameful. Not that I don't admit that I had looked through those alphabetical lists, each letter a thump at the heart as I'd moved my fingers down the column of names . . . Adams, James . . . Gambetti, Antonio . . . Harriet, Hyman . . . Jackson, Jeremiah. And then I would put my head down, my eyes fixed on a black boy that turned purple, until I'd closed my eyes and fell into sleep, the names rattling in my head until they moved into oblivion. My God, who wouldn't read those names, so many young men eagerly going and the scripting not even begun! So how could I condemn those who acted no differently than me? Well, there was indeed a winner. A young woman named Penelope Thompson who knew the young man and, once more, he was from New York. He was an aviator by the name of Edmond C. C. Genet. This crowd acted as though the state of New York had done something extraordinary and special.

I walked through the party, shaking hands and joining in on conversations that were as far away from war news as possible: The Divine Sarah Bernhardt was to perform soon and wasn't she just smashing; and who had seen the moving picture with Gish, or read Ring Lardner's new book *Gullible's Travels*, and wasn't that new song "When Shadows Fall" great? I succumbed to rye and more rye, so that I was absolutely famished when the spread was finally announced. The smoked salmon and asparagus and *petit pomme de terre* were wonderful. My tastes were heightened, I believe, by the anxiety of the occasion. I ate and drank like I knew deep down in my heart that this was going to be my last elaborate and enjoyable meal.

So, how does one say good-bye to a friend and hide the trembling fear of his death? Does one hold his hand too tightly or too long? Does one linger, searching his eyes for his future, hoping for sanctuary, a cool and delicate place to hide? Or should one rest a hand on his shoulder, saying you'll be back soon, really you will; or, I'm sure that Charlotte will wait for you? Do you tell him that he has his whole life in front of him, that he will see his children walk this earth and that he will absolutely die an old man? Empty words, but words that offer hope, so you might as well say them.

And this was what I did when I came to the crossroads of good-bye. I wrapped my arms around Charles' shoulder, pressed my head against his chest so that I could hear the soft thuds of his heart, and then I shut my eyes and tried to squeeze some of my life into his. I whispered this to him: *Be a brave soldier, the higher powers will be with you, I will think of you often with great kindness and genuine affection.* Then I walked away from him, knowing that the odds were simply against him, that Charlotte had absolutely no intention of waiting for him, that my seeing him again was beyond expectation. The Lord turn back the hands of time, pleaded Tennyson.

I left the windows of the car down as I drove back into the city. I needed to clear my head of the drink and food and sorrow of it all. But I felt free, like I could just drive and drive straight down to Palm Beach or to Asheville, join the rest of the hordes making their way to places were they could pretend that death did not come to us in the dead of night, or on the bow of a U-boat, or in ways we but dreamed in our most exasperating and cold moments. I wanted to speed up to the Smoky Mountains or down the silver, sandy roads of the south, my spirit soaring, free, free like Isadora Duncan when she let loose her body, unencumbered, her spirit bouncing off the walls of the Metropolitan, her life energy screeching in ecstasy, caring not a whit what anybody thought.

Was I ready for the responsibility of such freedom?

Let it be done, pronounced the Senate. The conscription was law in a 65 to 8 vote. All men between the ages of twenty-one and thirty had to declare themselves potential candidates for slaughter. This news increased the sales of the Doughboy Shoes at $11.50 a pair. As Billy Sunday continued to try and convince the world that Christ was coming, I couldn't help but wonder whether Jesus would wear Doughboys instead of sandals when he walked down Fifth Avenue leading the people's war, or through the trenches, or as he sits at the bargaining supper table with the great leaders when peace is negotiated. If this was to be a holy war, a new crusade, who would pursue the ghost of Bismarck through the Carpathian Mountains?

I felt that I was no longer simply me but much more; an uncoiling like a snake from its mother's egg. Who would understand what I was getting at if I'd pulled a chair to a table, ordered tea or whiskey and explained what was happening to me? Would you laugh, turn away from me, or say *yes, yes, I'm with you on that,* or have me hastily removed to see an alienist? But I would shout: do you not feel the ache in your chest when you know what to say, but cannot say it and just feel that if you do then who will be there to care or listen? It was like a pebble stuck in the gullet of a duck. It was that same feeling as when I'd read Joseph Conrad's new book *The Shadow Line.* It hit me like a lightning flash, as though this thing had waited for me all these last months, that it knew my search, that I was at last ready for the great adventure of life. Had Conrad written this just for me?

> *. . . the past eighteen months, . . . appeared a dreary, prosaic waste of days. I felt—how shall I express it—that there was not truth to be got out of them . . . I left it in that, to us, inconsequential manner in which a bird flies away from a comfortable branch. It was as though all unknowing I had heard a whisper or seen something. Well—perhaps! one day I was perfectly right and the next everything was gone glamour, flavour, interest, contentment—everything. It was one of those moments, you know. The green sickness of late youth descended on me and carried me off.*

That the war had changed New Yorkers should not be surprising, I suppose. Patriot, fighter, pacifist, unionite, prohibitionist, suffragette. It had caused a convergence of all kinds of opinions. The draft was placing a great strain on people, fueling bad feelings and hates. One night the Home Defense League Boys killed a young Negro. How incongruous was the name: The Home Defense League Boys. I didn't understand the specific reasons for the murder, and the news did not dare to tell the whole story. Why was it that these accounts told only part of the story, as though the short shrift of it was more convincing? Oh, then a riot ensued near Amsterdam Avenue and I heard that the authorities predicted that more riots were coming and more often. Race riot is what they called them. Why? The Negroes were joining the war. For too many of these young men, it was the best solution to their hunger. So what was the problem? They were acting as patriots, were they not? What was really sad in these stories was that these young men had no names. They passed quickly through this life and were *unidentified bodies.*

Elijah Rising

One of the incidents took place in the San Juan Hill District. That place then would have cast a pallor on any politician or any social reformer. But how many had made their way there? It was a dismal place, with poverty and bleakness right out of a Dickens novel. Obviously it had not been zoned. I was appalled by the tenements that jutted out into the sky, where in summer the heat seemed to penetrate the walls and stifle breathing. I had read about the northern migration of the Negro, but to see the consequences! What putrid dives were amassed and hidden in this city! But nothing would change with the war holding everyone's attention. We were not yet ready to cross the shadow line.

A little coal-black girl came up to me begging. She pulled my sleeve with her baby hand and smiled with a row of white teeth so wide and wondrous that her purple gums were lost to her dark skin. I reached deep into my pocket and gave her a hand full of coins. I heard throaty laughter and turned to a big woman sitting splay-legged on a stoop. *They's all be after yous, yous keep that up mista,* she said. And so I kept my hand out of my pockets and made a retreat, knowing that I would return. The dirty streets haunted me.

Mother returned from the theater just as I got home and I had to listen to her rave about the new play at The Republic. *You really should have come, Michael,* she preened. *Mr. Barrymore was exquisite as Peter Ibbetson and well, Constance was magnificent. You missed the after show reception.* I don't care about such things, I wanted to tell her. But I did not, for my plan was my own and I did not want to be thwarted. Why tip off the jailer before the get away?

The next day was Registration Day. The borders of the United States were closed so that no citizen of military age could escape. I steeled myself to tell Mother that I had been turned down for duty, for I knew she would ask me. But I was fortunate. She was out until the evening.

Anti-conscription agitation had started, but the cause was noiseless, muted by the new machines that would take us into the future. It was too late to stop the apocalyptic storm. The poor sots in the colleges had formed the Collegiate Anti-militarist League, called a bunch of "damned pacifists" by the "loyal elements." I was in sympathy with the peacemakers. Just the previous day the House of Representatives was given quite a show by Mister John Tilson of Connecticut. He had been in my house, I believe, several years ago. He was father's friend. What did he show that most deliberative body? A bomb! One that he proudly said would kill everything within a three-hundred-foot circle from where it fell. I had expected that learned, elected gentlemen in government would gasp, be appalled. But, it was hailed as an occasion marking progress. How many young men can fit into a circle encompassing three hundred feet? Those were the times that disputed Mr. Darwin. Please, sir, we have not evolved very far; the hunt had taken on another dimension.

I went back to San Juan Hill. I had seen papers tacked to buildings announcing a socialist protest meeting at Madison Square Garden. I decided to go. There were more police than speechmakers there. And it was rumored that many secret service men milled about the area. I wondered if I'd already knocked into a few. It was kind of frightening. The police had rifles and rode up and down the aisles with searchlights as though they were expecting, or maybe hoping, for violence. The speeches raged against the draft and were thus considered unpatriotic and seditious. Five people were arrested, including a pretty young woman by the name of Jennie Deimer, who was hauled away by two uniformed men. I did not understand her crime. After the spectacle, I left the Garden and took a trolley. I had lost my Madagascar so had to go bareheaded. I felt wonderful. I had taken the trolley and the subway and felt as though I were finally part of the rush of life. Pennsylvania Station had become both familiar and exciting. The train from Great Neck and back gave me a chance to see the people of the city. The little man at the ticket window looked at me as though I were a familiar site. A taxi man blubbered on and on about the war and victory and killing the Huns.

This is how the rich experience the war: Last night I was at last ready to tell Mother that was I leaving. But she'd gone to dinner at Churchill's, attending one of the patriotic reviews that had become the thing in dinning entertainment. When she came home she was escorted by several young men in Khaki uniform, their faces were flushed from the night air and too much liquor. And with them were their girls, all clothed in dresses that went up to their calves, spangles shimmered around their necks, and their mouths were painted dark red. They all looked the same, reflected like chimeras in the long Venetian mirror that adorned the library wall. They laughed unceasingly and begged mother to turn on the radio. "It's a Long Way to Tipperary" was blasting and I longed to escape the assault of the night. The young men twirled their girls around until midnight. Then they all kissed Mother on the cheek and yelled adieu and we're off to see the Kaiser. Mother was high in color, more than I had seen her in ages, as though the war had given her back her youth.

I decided to wait, let Mother expend her energy. *Oh, Michael,* she bubbled, *I've had a glorious day. Such brave young people!* And then she told me about her great triumph. *I've commissioned my agent to purchase as much property as possible from the Lorillard Spencer Estate near White Plains Road. Success*! she yelped. *Of the over one thousand lots available I am now the owner of two hundred. Do you*

know what will happen to property values in the future? she asked me. *Yes*, was all I could bring up. I waited for her to change into her green tea gown and make herself comfortable in her maroon embroidered chair. She unfolded the skirts of her gown and placed the shining cloth, fan-like, over her legs. She was turned toward the fireplace as though she already knew my purpose. The colors of the room whirled around me, each phantom at once distinct and separate, cold then hot. A fire in June was one of Mother's deviations and the roaring of the flames made me want to run away right then and there.

I let the cold from the marble seep through my jacket. I stood as straight as I could manage. Then I told her that I had presented myself to my country and had been rejected for physical reasons. My voice did not crack or tremble. I waited for the storm. It did not come.

I was given an alternative: I could become a gentlemen volunteer and join the ambulance corps like many young men who were seeking romance in war. *Enlist in the corps*, she said, *and you shall be a savior to the dying. I cannot save the dead*, I said. *The requirements are minimal, Michael, less than for the regular army, and you must be at least 5 feet 4 inches. Surely*, she insisted, *you can meet those requirements. Playing lawn tennis at Princeton*, I replied, *is not exactly a great recommendation for war.*

She slowly turned and looked at me, a not unkind smile spreading across her cheeks: *Well, Michael, we each must do what we must. I must apologize if I have protected you too much from the world. Perhaps one day we will understand each other. I wish you well in your life. Know that*

Lyn LeJeune

I will always be here for you. Should you need anything before you leave, let me know. Your allowance will be continued. Do not worry about your Father; it all comes from me, anyway. She glided to me and kissed me lightly on the cheek then left the room.

I was amazed, thinking that families are made up of aliens, that members make war sometimes and then peace comes, even if it is only a truce, and then we each go our separate ways. It is better, this, than a killing.

I left my old home with my valises and headed toward Greenwich Village. I was determined to enter the whirlwind life of O'Neil and Eastman and the pacifists and socialists and Emma Goldman and maybe I would have great luck and meet my hero John Reed. I found a flat on Washington Square, not far from where John Reed had once lived and still makes appearances. My flat had three rooms: a bedroom, a small kitchen, and a little room for my study. The summer had been hotter than usual, but I left the one window open and enjoyed the soft breezes of the night. The sounds of children playing in the street and adults discussing their routines of life made me smile. But most of all, it was a throaty saxophone, its melody floating from a far away cellar, that finally hinted that there would be an end of loneliness for me. My books were piled to my waist in four corners and I read until my eyes burned with both joy and remorse for the years I had given to the surface of this world. The aroma of new foods played in the air. My stomach pains were gone. No more tutti frutti pepsin gum for occasional bouts of dyspepsia! I would eat sausage and spaghetti and, in one little restaurant I know about, taste horsemeat. My clothes were wrinkled. I wore short sleeves. I took a bath whenever I wanted to. I enjoyed the simple pleasures of life.

I went to New York's east side. Harlem was vibrant with people from all over the world. Italians and Germans and Russians and Jews and Negroes and pacifists and socialists and even anarchists. Were these the aliens that America feared? I walked from 96th Street to 129th, then to Lexington and Madison, and the different languages bombarded me like particles of gold falling from the heavens. The cadences fell at my feet, paving my way. I knew what people were looking for when they left their homes to come here. I had found the treasure, too.

Every other day I'd go to the Liberal Club. If I waited long enough I'd see and hear more in one day than all the newspapers could tell. One

43

day, Emma Goldman distributed the *Blast*. I sat casually, pushed my chair back, drank strong coffee, watched the comings and goings, and listened to speeches against the conscript, for revolution, against the war, for the women's suffrage. It was so easy to belong there.

On a hot day in June, I cannot remember the exact day now, Emma was hauled away by the police. The charge was treason, seditious speech, disloyalty; they were all the same, it seemed. I admired Emma's stoic good humor during the ordeal. She smiled, walked with her head held high, and with a flash of purple (her favorite color) she turned to her friends and waved good-bye. After I watched the authorities drive away with Emma, I walked downtown to Billy Sunday's Tabernacle. Was he still recruiting souls and pitching them across the street? Billy was leaving New York, taking a train westward in search of new souls, so I yelled to his departing train *go to it, Billy*! From the recruiting station, I heard music that ground out words that were not words. Another new song rang out: *Oh! how she could yacki, hacki, wicki, wacki, woo...*

On a clear afternoon, my dream came true. I met John Reed. The news pictures made him look small and distressed. But in person he was tall and handsome. His black hair was slicked back in a wet wave that caught the bright blue shadows of low-hanging light bulbs. He turned his head in laughter, from one friend and admirer to another. They called him Jack. His ears stuck out a bit, and I imagined that he was constantly listening to the sorrows of the world. I wanted to join in the discussion, but I just couldn't get the gumption up. But I was close enough to hear that *The Masses* had been stopped by the government because it was considered seditious under the new Espionage Act. Jack stood up on a chair and said that the capitalists of America had tricked the people into war and that the common man all over the world had guns placed in their hands without being asked. *The world revolution is at hand*, he shouted, *and we must all be prepared to participate. How can we be happy*, he asked the group around him, as he threw his arms out, *when our happiness is built on the misery of others? Do you eat because others go hungry? Do you have clothes in the winter when others freeze from nakedness?* He spoke about the Russian Revolution and the hope of the proletariat. He vowed that he would go to Russia and return to spread the cause of revolution to the world. The group cheered in anticipation of seeing him off across the ocean. I could see in the eyes of these young people a sort of envy for his bravery. They would never have the courage to go with him.

When Jack stood up to leave, I tapped him on the shoulder. He turned, smiled, looked into my eyes and grasped my left shoulder. *Michael, have faith, my man,* he whispered. *There're plenty causes for all of us.* And then he was gone.

I walked by the Long Island Station one morning. A crowd of girls was bidding adieu to their men. I watched as the train took the soldiers to Camp Upton at Yaphank, Long Island, where once upon a time lovers passed time on picnics. The girls were dressed to the nines; spring dresses, sleeves flapping in the wind as they waved and blew red kisses that stained their white gloves. And on their heads they still wore those horrid little round hats with veils that looked like the barbed wire of the western front, a mysterious covering for beauty, something for the men to remember them by.

I listened to the train whistle echo through the streets: the Germans were offering $100.00 for the first dead American, and the socialist press has asked why conscription was necessary if this war was so popular.

I received my allowance at the post every first Monday of the month. Sometimes Mother sent me a note. The news was sad. Two friends had died. Pepi was our Pekinese and had been with the family for more than ten years. He died quite suddenly, found by Hilda in the pantry one morning. Mother had him buried in the Westchester Cemetery for pets. A family friend, Samuel Lockleed, had been killed, perhaps by cannon fire, or disease, no one was quite sure. *Samuel is dead* was all she wrote in thick black ink rapidly scrawled across shiny white paper. The dark blue letters *M. C. H.* were branded across the top of the page.

The latest news was that 202,669 men had joined up since April.

My flat was cold day and night now. I went down to Gimble's and bought a new wool suit on sale for $16.50 It would be my last for a long time, since wool was the fabric of uniforms. Fuel was in short supply. Many of the tenants in my building gathered newspapers from the streets to be used for fuel. Mrs. O'Malley had a stack that reached over her head, and she was taller than me. She muttered constantly about the coming hard winter. The government began to ration food. Officials predicted that more than half of our food supplies would be depleted if ice blocked the waterways. Half of what was available would go to the war effort. Mr. Hoover had taken over wartime food sources and on every street corner posters were tacked up with this announcement: *Food Will Win the War*. I understood that we could not let the boys starve. But just five blocks from my flat there were slums filled with hungry, crying children.

Depressed by it all, I treated myself to the moving pictures this afternoon. *Rasputin: The Black Monk* was at the Pantheon and for 25 cents it was an entire afternoon of entertainment. I was enthralled with the picture shows. They brought a world of war right to our sights, convinced the people of what was true or false, what they should or should not think. I believed that these moving pictures would change the world. I wondered what Jack Reed, sojourning in Russia, thought about Rasputin and the movies.

The lights of Broadway went out at 11 P.M. by order of the Fuel Administration. So the people in the Village got together and held a *Moon Dance*. Little boys ran up and down the streets handing out invitations: *Come at moon-up and stay till sun-up*. It was great! Jazz band music floated in the air, and I danced down the sidewalk with beautiful girls whose faces were hidden by the dark. Liquor poured from every pocket and purse, and I drank so that the cold air did not bother me. Just before dawn I returned to my flat and lit candles and lay in my bed watching the shadows dance on the wall. I saw dead ghosts fighting life and then I fell fast asleep and dreamt nothing.

Next day, the talk up and down the street and in the Liberal Club was not about the war in Europe, but the war in Washington, the fight for women's suffrage. Miss Lucy Burns of New York, who had spoken on the suffrage amendment, had been jailed in Washington and sentenced to serve six months. Just for picketing the White House!

German prisoners are treated better than those women. They were being kept at Fort Douglas in Utah. Some were spies, some were even gunboat commanders, the ones who blew up American ships. They were given decent housing, a hospital, a motion-picture theater, and a chapel. The women who were arrested had their clothes taken away; they were manacled and refused visitors and their children and even their lawyers.

Miss Burns was even threatened with being placed in a straitjacket. Do they think women who want to vote are insane?

On 107th Street and Park Avenue, at the Star Casino, representatives of the I.W.W. delivered speeches requesting aid for compatriots arrested for antiwar activities. The police were there in full force. I was warned by a fellow standing next to me to watch for Secret Service men. *What does one look like*, I asked. *Got me*, he said. It was calm about fifteen minutes into the speeches. Then the speakers turned to a different tune, urging support of the Bolsheviki and their bid for peace. I was at a loss to understand how the Bolsheviki could bring peace. I read, even in Jack Reed's articles, that the Russian people were starving. Lenine and Trotsky had done with Kerensky and all hell had broken loose. So, the speeches did not make much sense to me. But I stayed and listened and especially agreed, finally, with Miss Elizabeth Freeman, who simply urged peace, peace, peace, now! As I headed home, a young boy handed me a circular announcing a dance in the park celebrating Lenine. I knew that I would not be there.

I learned how to stay warm. My flat was impossible to heat and the winter was creeping into the walls. The landlord told me that coal was hard to come by and that we must all prepare for a bad winter. So I went to the moving picture matinee to see the opening of *Les Miserables*. It was called a picturization of the classic work. An actor named William Farnum depicted Jean Val Jean. Well, I liked it so much that I went back for the eight-thirty showing

The next day was 7 December 1917. America declared war on Austria-Hungary. Rodin had died on November 25.

As I fumbled to the Metropolitan Museum, service flags flapped in the cold air, the stars that marked each perished serviceman were like bullets igniting with each hard flap, flap, flap. My face became raw with the unrelenting cold and the weight I had lost made my heavy coat feel like hands pulling me down. I stared, it seemed, for hours at Rodin's figures, seeing but not seeing them, although I had studied his sculptures many times before. I waited until they were burned black into my mind and I walked away with the memory. I could stand it no more, the death of this great man, so I scurried to the new J wing, filled with classical sculptures. I entered upon the great lion of the 5th century, which took up a central place. It was there by design of the gods or the curators, I did not know which. But it was for our time. It was called *Fighting Gaul*. I left the warmth of the museum. The news at the exit sign was that Mr. J.P. Morgan had announced a gift of seven million dollars in art to the Met.

When I got back, a letter was stuck in the door. It was in her straight cursive hand. She was going to winter in Florida and will be staying at the Royal Poinciana. She complained about the lack of coal in the city and has decided to shut the house up, except for the kitchen and servant rooms. She wrote: *I cannot bear the Hooverization of the food in the New York restaurants one more night, so will be off to better places. If I have to eat one more oyster, I shall die!* She added more than four thousand dollars to my regular allowance and wrote that I should perhaps find better lodgings.

Someone knocked on my door. I opened it and a young boy thrust a package at me. It was wrapped in shiny green and red paper, with a small teddy bear noosed by a candy cane ribbon. I opened it, careful not to tear the paper. To say I was astounded and overjoyed is an understatement. First, that Mother would give me this present and second, that I could not have asked for anything that I needed more at that moment of my life. The first published volume of Leo Tolstoi's *Journals* lay in my hands. I stroked the cover until I felt heat on the leather, then I held it to my chest.

I read until the electricity went out and then I lit a candle, my finger following each word until the end. Like me, Tolstoi had been unhappy with his life and his surroundings and wanted to give up the luxuries and comforts that material things brought. He struggled with the needs of his soul. He knew what was right: That he should give up his wealth and social position and share in the life of the destitute who surrounded his family estate. *To flee*, he had written. *To flee!* Then I noticed a sheaf of paper lying on the floor. Another note from Mother. *PS: It is sad, but I read that the peasant mobs in Russia have burned Count Tolstoi's chateau, destroying much of his original writings. Love, Mother.*

The next day was Christmas and the Tree of Light was turned on at Madison Square Garden at five o'clock. Bitter cold had enveloped the city. Ice had formed on the lakes and waterways, preventing the delivery of coal. I listened to the 347th Infantry, which was composed of all Negroes, sing with joy and hope, then I watched the lights flicker until I smelled fire and burning rubber. It reminded me of incense. I walked to the subways, making my detours and routes, until I reached twenty-second street and the Association for Improving the Condition of the Poor. *The Times* had just come out with the city's yearly Christmas list of the neediest cases. The appeal was for one dollar, or five, or one hundred or more. A pretty young woman sat behind an old desk, her head and hands covered against the cold. I could not tell where it was coldest, in the building or out. She greeted me with a *Merry Christmas, Sir*, and I handed her an envelope, saying *Merry Christmas to you, too*. In the envelope was four thousand dollars.

THE BARBARIANS

Lord, I just can't keep from cryin'
—Blind Willie Johnson

Elijah Rising

My Mama used to tell me that we all lived this life broken. I just had to make the best of it. Black was the color of my skin *and ain't nobody gonna skin youse alive and make you white. They might skin youse alive,* she'd laugh, *but dat ain't gonna make youse white. Gonna make youse bleed.* Through all the years traveling from New York into Texas, I had my Mama with me. I heard her voice, she guided me, I touched her Bible and the words poured from my mouth. I was once called The Black Preacher on a Fiery Cross, and I think Mama would have been proud of me. I owe her my life.

And I owe Hiram Bell because he taught me how to preach, how to pick just the right words for the occasion. I forgive him for his betrayal. And Michael, my poor Michael, I owe him money, transportation, and his belief in me. I knew from the start he wanted something I could not give him, something that the Lord would not permit. The times were always against me, and they always will be. But for Michael, there will never be a time to be against. I cannot save him from the barbarians.

From the time I stepped off that freight train in Memphis, it had always been about one thing; abiding my time until the barbarians caught up with me. I wanted them; I needed them; without their hate and tempestuousness, I would never become the true and great Elijah. The effective Elijah. The Lord pointed the way, gave me strength, and directed them to me.

I suppose I should tell you about the barbarians. Who they were, what they were up to. But you already know them. All you have to do is stop on a clear afternoon, when the sun blazes hot on your head and you have no hat for want of a few pennies. You think back, and the years loop around you and youcannot find the beginning of your life. You see him coming, he is like a swift gliding bird, like the peregrine falcon. Stop, watch him come in for a landing; his wings wide and strong as though with one flap he can stop the winds; he lands, he junglewalks, and he finds the mice and living things that will make his meal for the day. The falcon is a creature of the Lord, but he is made in the image of the barbarians. Or are the barbarians made in His image? I cannot know which. He is your father, the one who strapped you until the blood ran down your legs and your Mama cried but did nothing; he is your Mama who did nothing; he is the head of empires, the one who makes war for the sake of war and booty; he is the small conqueror who follows orders; he is the money changer in the temple; he is the boss who refused you work because of the color of your skin or the slant of your eyes or the thing between your legs; he is the fire marshal who took bribes and the entire shirt factory burned and burned and the women died sewing the shirts for the rich. I cannot go on. You get the idea; you know who your own personal barbarians are. Remember that they are Legion.

I want to say something else at the beginning of this part of my story. As I sped through life, often too fast, I missed many things. But I saw millions of images and voices and I learned. When I am preaching, when you see a photograph of me in the papers, I am sure you assume that I am an ignorant man. But I am not. How surprised Michael was when I quoted Tennyson. How surprised you would be to know that I see the barbarians of the past, the ones that Rome blamed for its demise. The Goths and the

Vandals and the Celts. Which ones do you think will bring this American empire down? Barbarians are known to amass and grow from one idea, one word. I learned that from Billy Sunday. Watch the eyes of the people, the slant of their heads, the wanness of their skin. See the many who have not eaten for days and come to a preacher to ask God for sustenance. They prayed themselves, but nothing had happened. Wait until the right moment and then all you have to do is blame the barbarians for your plight. It is the black man, it is the government, it is the union, it is the strikebreaker, it is the president, it is the Indian, it is everyone you can think of that is not deserving of a plate of meat. Tell them that. Use the word retribution and they will sway this way and that and then all it takes is one word to bring the crowd to your corner. It is the corner of hate. I overcame the hate and tried for love. Often, you know what is right when you know what is wrong.

When I was in New York, before the time of Michael, I found a purse full of money, a diamond ring, and a gun. You might think this was a tremendous find for a poor black boy. But here was the problem. If I tried to sell the diamond they'd think I'd stolen it and off I'd go to jail. If I carried the gun, well, into The Tombs with me. And then it came to the money. Small bills, I was fortunate for that. So I threw away the purse, along with the diamond and the gun and off I went to spend one dollar for food for Mama. I should have known not to let the bulge in my pants pocket stick out. I smelled fresh bread and the brine of pickled fish. Hurry,

hurry, I puffed and ran to Stein's Emporium. I bought a loaf of bread, two fishes, and a bag of candy and headed home to Mama. And then the barbarians got me. See, they're everywhere. It was two boys with whom I had played in the garbage-strewn field next to Potter's Field. I felt a clunk on my head and the blood ran down in my eyes. They pushed me and stomped me and a little hand wiggled in my pants and then they were gone. See this scar on the side of my head? It is only one of my souvenirs from the barbarians. The other, as you may remember, is a piece of branch from brother's hanging tree.

Oh, I could go on, but you understand what I am trying to tell you. Beware the barbarians, they are all around you. Beware, they come in the guise of the gatekeepers.

I carried Mama's Bible because that is was I was made of. Scripture and words upon words. I read many books in my life, *Moby Dick* for example, because I understood obsession. (I know what you are thinking, reader, that this black boy surely was a miracle. You are right, and everyday of my life I resisted my abilities. Until that one day, which you will hear about later, I accepted my fits of genius and ability to remember word for word everything I read). Read this and you will understand possession as well as the undercurrent that is the barbarian.

> *In his infallible wake, though; but follow the wake that's all. Helm there; steady, as thou goest, and hast been going. What a lovely day! Were it a new-made world, and made for a summer-house to the angels, and this morning the first of its throwing open to them, a fairer day could not dawn upon the world. Here's food for thought, had Ahab time to think; but Ahab never thinks; he only feels, feels, feels; that's tingling enough for mortal man! To think is audacity. God only has the right and privilege. Thinking is, or ought to be, a coolness and a calmness; and our poor hearts throb, and our poor brains beat too much for that. And yet, I've sometimes thought my brain was very calm,*

Lyn LeJeune

*frozen calm, this old skull cracks so, like a glass in which
the contents turned to ice, and shiver it.*

When I jumped and acted somewhat like a monkey on stage, I was calm inside, calculating, audacious, becoming a barbarian.

I could accomplish nothing in the metropolis. Mama had gone to her maker and I hopped a train. I knew the colors of dusk out there in the wilderness. I had seen the violet swatches across the sky as I prayed near Mama's body. I knew that when I entered Canaan the sun would hang low and weighty over the horizon, the rays would glint in the flowing clear streams making sparkles of heavenly light. Little Liza once thought those were the fireflies she'd heard about, but they were not. I told her those were signals for the Lord just for her, that happy times were coming, that she would grow to womanhood and have children and those children would have children and so on and on and she would be remembered as the mother of them all. And then that night I took her out in the fields and showed her the real fireflies and cautioned her not to kill them, not to put them in a jar, for their lives were short and they had been given the privilege of the plains. *Let them be,* I told her. *Let all living things be.*

The moment I saw the Red River, I knew I was entering the Land of Canaan. I knew we had to go southward into Texas and across the Missouri River and to the Brook of Egypt into the Jordon River Valley. That was when Michael bought the car and truck and it was also then that I knew that the Lord had sent him, my left hand, to bring me out of Egypt. I saw far into the future to a place called California, and there would be the Promised Land and it was called Hollywood and I would be like Asa, Al Jolson, on Broadway, only I'd be a real black man. Dreamers we all are and then we become barbarians. Sing with me:

When Israel was in Egypt's land: Let my people go,
Oppress'd so hard they could not stand, Let my People go.
Go down, Moses,
Way down in Egypt land,
Tell old Pharaoh,
Let my people go.

Elijah Rising

When young Smith was murdered I was not surprised. It was the reaction of the children that was heartbreaking. Liza fell to the ground and sobbed and all of the others fell after her. They wailed in the wind, shook the branches of the trees, the water stopped flowing, the earth stopped turning. All this magic, all this halting nature for the death of a child. We lifted him from the water, blood seeped from his head. *Don't turn him over*, I told Michael. *The children have enough to remember.* Mama Jones wrapped him in a blue blanket and we carried him off for quick burial. John brought the bag of lime and Smith was laid to rest, as the saying goes. But I did not think that this child would rest, because I was sure he did not see his murderers. Killed from behind; barbarians are always cowards.

There was Liza, John, Miller, Jackson, Violet, Rose and Laz. None of them were over fifteen. Mama Jones put them to an early bed and wiped away their tears and song *Go Down, Go down to the river and let my people go. Go down, bend your head, and let my people go. Go Down . . .* Michael stumbled away and sat behind the truck, his head between his knees. This is what had always entranced me about Michael; how someone who suffered so little, at least compared to my people, could feel such utter despair. I knew there were reasons beyond my wanting to know. Perhaps, in the end, I could have saved him. Yet I often turned away and made busy with my other concerns.

Mama Jones pulled me down to sit on a large boulder next to her. *'Lijah, you be in a big mess o' trouble,* she said. *I tell ya tings as I see um. You be full of pride and dat's wat's gonna kill ya. Be not likened to Obadiah.*

I know all about Obidiah, I know I follow him into the wilderness and on to the destruction of this country. But it is only in following the damned, Mama, that we can see the wrong path. Obidiah was a prophet.

You tink you be a prophet sir? And so you cain't no mo talk o' pride den the devil.

Only Mama Jones could set me straight sometimes. I was prideful and Michael would do anything I asked of him and beyond. Women, women of all sizes, colors, opinions, will be the real saviors of the world.

But I had to prove myself and so I recited from The Book of Obadiah:

Lyn LeJeune

Thus saith the Lord Jehovah concerning Edom: We have heard tidings from Jehovah, and an ambassador is sent among the nations, saying, Arise ye, and let us rise up against her in battle. Behold, I have made thee small among the nations: thou art greatly despised. The pride of thy heart hath deceived thee, O thou that dwellest in the clefts of the rock, whose habitation is high; that saith in his heart, Who shall bring me down to the ground? Though thou mount on high as the eagle, and though thy nest be set among the stars, I will bring thee down from thence, saith Jehovah. If thieves came to thee, if robbers by night (how art thou cut off!), would they not steal only till they had enough? if grape-gatherers came to thee, would they not leave some gleaning grapes? How are the things of Esau searched! How are his hidden treasures sought out! All the men of thy confederacy have brought thee on thy way, even to the border: the men that were at peace with thee have deceived thee, and prevailed against thee; they that eat thy bread lay a snare under thee: there is no understanding in him. : Shall I not in that day, saith Jehovah, destroy the wise men out of Edom, and understanding out of the mount of Esau? And thy mighty men, O Teman, shall be dismayed, to the end that every one may be cut off from the mount of Esau by slaughter. For the violence done to thy brother Jacob, shame shall cover thee, and thou shalt be cut off for ever. In the day that thou stoodest on the other side, in the day that strangers carried away his substance, and foreigners entered into his gates, and cast lots upon Jerusalem, even thou wast as one of them. But look not thou on the day of thy brother in the day of his disaster, and rejoice not over the children of Judah in the day of their destruction; neither speak proudly in the day of distress. Enter not into the gate of my people in the day of their calamity; yea, look not thou on their affliction in the day of their calamity, neither lay ye hands on their substance in the day of their calamity. And stand thou not in the crossway, to cut off those of his that escape; and deliver not

57

up those of his that remain in the day of distress. For the day of Jehovah is near upon all the nations: as thou hast done, it shall be done unto thee; thy dealing shall return upon thine own head. For as ye have drunk upon my holy mountain, so shall all the nations drink continually; yea, they shall drink, and swallow down, and shall be as though they had not been. But in mount Zion there shall be those that escape, and it shall be holy; and the house of Jacob shall possess their possessions. And the house of Jacob shall be a fire, and the house of Joseph a flame, and the house of Esau for stubble, and they shall burn among them, and devour them; and there shall not be any remaining to the house of Esau; for Jehovah hath spoken it. And they of the South shall possess the mount of Esau, and they of the lowland the Philistines; and they shall possess the field of Ephraim, and the field of Samaria; and Benjamin shall possess Gilead. And the captives of this host of the children of Israel, that are among the Canaanites, shall possess even unto Zarephath; and the captives of Jerusalem, that are in Sepharad, shall possess the cities of the South. And saviours shall come up on mount Zion to judge the mount of Esau; and the kingdom shall be Jehovah's.

I smiled at my memory. Mama Jones touched me on the shoulder, used me to pull herself up, and walked away without turning back. But I saw her shake her heard as though she had heard Satan's trumpets call me to hell. For pride I shall be punished; it is the sin of all sins, it travels through wormwood and infects the souls of the righteous.

One day Michael came back from town with a brown bag under his arms. It was tied with twine and had my name written across it in red. He looked as though he had swallowed ten purple martins. He handed me the package and said: *I thought you could use a new one.* After all we had been through, after all the preaching and jumping and quoting and seeing the dead gone and buried, the idiot gives me a spanking copy of The New

Lyn LeJeune

Testament. Now which one was I to choose? The old or the new. I opened the book to a random page and first line I saw was: *The poor man is hated even by his own neighbor, / But the rich has many friends.*

    This book is a lie, I said. *The barbarians wrote this book.*

CROSSING THE SHADOW LINE

My journey was done and behind me lay hill and dale, and Life and Death.
How shall man measure progress there where the dark-faced Josie lies?
—W.E.B. DuBois

Elijah Rising

I needed to buy a typewriter. My hands were frozen to my pen. I walked the streets for material, the stuff of life. How could I write stories from what *my* life had been?

She was found in the hallway, on the third story, the windows of the tenement fastened with black oil paper to keep out the cold. But it seeped in and ice encased the windows. She had come to 325 West 37th Street, a freed slave, escaping a land that threw her away with promises that would not be kept. She was old, very old. I looked down at her and knew that this real death would make a good story. Tell the world about what is really going on, I thought. A lady from the relief workers society had reported the death to the authorities and had called a wagon to take the body away. I asked the lady for a statement. All she said was: *Unidentified Negro woman.*

The tenements were like catacombs. I walked by them, through them, and around them so often that at night I dreamed I was buried alive. I had asked the relief worker to take me with her on her visits. Most often it was just to touch a baby's face or give the mother a ration card for milk or coarse flour. The ration continued especially since the New York harbors were still icebound. We were trapped. I took notes, word-sketching the faces I saw, noting the languages and speech patterns; most often no English was spoken. It was a world with boarded windows, where ripped pieces of cardboard boxes flapped with the wind. Where old blankets and straw mattresses were stained by love and sickness and birth. One morning I saw a child holding an orange.

I loved the raw faces of the people. I had seen the faces of the men on street corners in the light of day or after dark in bars. I learned to like beer; rye was hard to find. These common men talked about the past as though the future would not come. They had accepted their destinies. Their god did not look kindly upon New York. It was March and two weeks before a hurricane had descended on the city, sending hard winds and wild rain through the streets. Trucks turned over and people grabbed at anything that would secure them to the world. The world thawed, but the cold came back furious and mean. Nature was bullying us into submission.

March, 1918 and things were falling apart. The Liberal Club was devastated. The Creel Committee had come down hard on their publications. Max Eastman was on the run. The pressures of war had taken sympathy away from the workers. The mail services chose what would be sent out. Emma Goldman and Alexander Berkman were charged with sedition and sent to federal prison. The only newspapers left on the streets were the "acceptable" ones. One of the newest ones, *Hearst's Magazine*, came out with its first headline: Harry Lander's *Story of the War*. It was a romantic rendition of the First World War. But Brentano's bookstore was still open. I picked up Upton Sinclair's *The Jungle* and Zane Grey's new book *The U.P. Trail* then went to the Broadway Theatre to see *Tarzan and the Apes*.

I went home and outlined five stories: Joshua, Madrid, Helen, Samuel, and Hannah. All Children. A knock on my door and there was my monthly allowance sent by special carrier. Then I wrote about Joshua:

He is eight years old. His parents were born in Romania. They came to America in 1902, but were unable to name the country of their birth because the continent of Europe had been shattered by war. They had no home, no hope, until Joshua was born on American soil. Then the mother died of dysentery. The father works as a laborer on the docks. Joshua sells papers on the street corners to make enough money to buy food. He is a victim of the fight between the big newspapers and the independent distributors over who will get the cut in sales Joshua is a newsboy. He is used.

In the spring, the rain falls on the heads of our enemies. Children recognize that phenomenon before anyone else; it is what makes things even out. And so it is with young Joshua Berkowitz, stooped before his time, wise beyond his years. Dirt gives his skin a brownish hue. His hair is the color of henna and sticks out from his black tattered cap. Between his rumbling coughs he yells paper, gets youse paper hea! Below his left eye is a softening bruise, turned green since last week, the result of his refusal to pay double. He fights knowing that he will not win.

My first story ran for twelve pages, typed by a young woman who had set up her business at the end of Delancey Street. Her name was

Elijah Rising

Melba. I posted the story to *Vanity Fair*. I never heard back. But there was news, the American army had taken Bellau Woods.

I heard someone whisper; the barbarians are coming.

Time passed. It was July. The heat burned the earth. Children played in the streets, their bare feet oblivious to the hot bricks. My world had shrunk to the East Side. I believed that I was happy. I wrote another story, this time about Madrid.

> *She is a dark sprite, fragile, luminous, and will not survive these times. Around her neck she wears the symbol of her faith, intended to protect her during her journey through this world. It is better made for eternity. Her mother named her after the place of her family's beginnings. Generations of Spaniards bred and thrived in the hills outside of Madrid. Her people were not only dark, but ruddy, their leathery skin absorbing the sun as a necessity of their lives. Madrid does not thrive in the new country. Her color is too deep to vanish in the shaded streets. Her thin skin is pocked from an illness acute to civilization. That Madrid would succumb to the overcrowding and lack of clean air was already known to her mother. The father had died in a railroad accident, crushed between two cold cars. The child turns the rope over and over, singing a song of one and two pence and roses and cockle shells. Madrid does not have the energy to be the jumper and she wonders what are pences and what are cockle shells.*

I read over my work then a thought came to me*: Loneliness is a disease.* This disturbed me, so I went to Sultan Street, interviewed people from other countries and sampled Hungarian food. Then I went to the deepest slums of New York.

Lyn LeJeune

He was so small, so dirty, and he should have been filled with anger. But he was not; he was as clean inside as any man could hope to be. I called him Little Washington. He appeared when my life seemed an ungainly spiral, a void, my days sorely numbered, when I needed either redemption or salvation. I saw him in my mind as though he were a vision come to save me. There he was scuttling down the cavernous alley of this metropolis, this New York City, moving as fast as a little brown rat. Some would have called his demeanor repulsive, bandy-legged, another weight on the body politic. He was a little black boy and surely he was from the south. So many had come north, looking of jobs, for a warm bed, for someone to say *welcome, you are part of this great country*. But I knew what *they* saw; only the silhouette, the trappings, those babbling shadows that had bothered the well-off for so long. It was 1918 and the world was still in bitter turmoil. So why should anyone care about Little Washington? But to my eyes he was blithe and angelic and divine, all substance and form, like the force of a good dream. I had followed him for two weeks and knew that I had to get his words down precisely, to convey the mood, the horror of it all. I thought that melancholy was the word for which I searched, the ambience I needed to inject into my writing so that I could clearly draw his life. How does a writer make the reader empathize with the subject, and then faithfully execute the words so that they are like arrows in the people's heart? Ah, democracy! in which the writer's duty is to lift the heavy weight of disillusionment from the shoulders of the common man.

I did not lessen Little Washington when I wrote about him in the exact patterns and syntax of his speech. I caught him stealing, placed my hand on his arm, and handed him a dollar. He smiled at me, slipped the money from my hand and followed me to an alley where we sat on wooden boxes. I asked why he stole. Of course he was defensive, his black eyes flashing this way and that, as though he expected the New York police to suddenly appear. I assured him I was alone and merely wished to speak with him. *I am a student of humanity*, I said to him. He only laughed and said: *I ain't one o them men likes*. I told him to just tell me why he needed to steal and that I would give him five dollars for his story. I assured him that my intentions were just that and no more.

I don't want anything from you but your story. Straight as an arrow, I said.

Elijah Rising

His gaze fixed on a movement at the end of the alley. *Look, so I stoles the bread, he said. So what. I's been doing it fa three weeks now and ain't got caught yet. Man Fuslage, the old bastard cain't see anyway. His stow's just round the corner from our place. A one-room basement cold as shit and wet. And I beats the rats to death every night. I's afraid they's chew on Mama while she dreaming her bad shaking dreams. Lil May died last month. She was a bit. Like a little gray bird too hongry to live. The stealing thing is easy. I's planning on perfecting sausages next. They's all laid out in the morning, so it easy to jes go byand grab 'em. Gotta be quick as a jack. Mama has a weakness fo sweets, so I's figuring to move on to the big shops. I gots my eye on those candies in gold boxes fore the doctor say the pleurisy and the liver takes her away. Our daddy, I think that's what he must o been, whipped us something fierce. Broke our skin here and there, just to be mean. He's long gone and good riddance. There was ol aunt Betty who jes sat and watched the fire. Watched and never did say one damn word again after dem bunch o boys took her out to yonder field. She's just cry and cry and then yell every time the church bell rangs. She up an killed herself las spring. So, there's only me soon as Mama goes, soon as I get her dem gold chocolates.*

He bent his head forward and looked at me and licked his lips. *Is dat 'nough fo ya?*

How did you even get to New York? I asked.

I come wid ma ma and sista; In the summer of 1917.

He stopped talking for a while, his eyes closed as though he were summoning a story that I knew would not be true. His father, he said, was killed in St. Louis, Illinois. *By a mob they call it, yes, a mob trying to get rid of da black mans who been hired to work in munitions plants. Like I tol you,* he continued, *I been with dem union people's here in New York, been rounded up by the city bosses. Hell, all dey want is a decent work. But me, I make more money filching. Sausages fo supper. I'm telling you sho. Now were's that money you promised me?*

I gave him the money and he agreed to meet me again for ten dollars.

Our second interview was at two-thirty in the afternoon, in a park area, second bench from the entrance. I brought him a chocolate cake that was freshly baked that very morning by a bakery frequented by the servants of the rich. Mother's maid, Eloise, made Tuesday and Thursday morning trips there. Fresh cakes were demanded by Mother; stout and big-boned, her bosom jutting out from her chest like the lady on the bow of a ship, throwing orders at the servants. I haven't seen her in ages. Well, I suppose I wanted Little Washington to taste the possibilities right off. Or was I bringing him rising expectations? How sad though, a mere chocolate cake and I was worrying that I'd make the poor kid a Marxist.

He did not walk but sauntered toward me. He was such a sallow child already, with arms like broken twigs. His blackness was almost hidden by the yellow tinge of his skin. He came toward me like a little ghost. The air had been sucked from the atmosphere and only dry, barren heat remained. His filthy shirt, once white, was opened and flapping gently as he bounced on the hard path. His dark, shiny skin was reflected by the sun and shimmered the bony ribs of a baby. His pants were colorless, loose, tied to his body by a bail rope. He wore misshapen shoes without laces. Were they enough to keep the hookworms away, I thought. I heard rumbling and I looked to the west where the sky was dark and heavy. He wasn't more than ten years old it seemed and I was afraid that he would die hanging from the prickly branches, while this nation gave birth to ignoramuses. My urge was to protect him; but I could not change him into something the world would accept. Not yet, at least. So how did I go about helping without pretending to be some damned false emancipator. Who exactly did I think I was?

I moved to the right side of the bench, giving him as wide an area to sit so he would be comfortable. I put the bright white box with the chocolate cake just at the exact spot so that it would evenly be between us. It was my way of inviting him to sit with me. I had never seen him sit. He seemed always ready for flight, always bound for another place as though he were lost and trying to find his way. Well, I suppose he was.

Little Washington sat down, but did not look at me. He stared at the box. Then he smiled and opened the box. *You keeps ya promise, mista*, he said. *I's hongry as a new mama.* He reached into the pocket of his tattered pants. It was a hound's tooth pattern and I wondered where he'd pinched it. A soup spoon emerged, silver against his ashen gray skin. I remember that it was getting on to evening and the light of the world was blocked by the rickety buildings around us. Little Washington held the spoon in the air like it was a divining rod, then he closed his eyes and chanted: . . . *to the gods of cake, potatoes, whiskey and babies with lost souls, I bless this here cake. Amen.* The spoon glided downward like an elegant metallic kite and plunged into the edge of the cake. The brown emulsion rose and entered his mouth. For that moment he was in heaven. I watched in fascination as he ate about a fourth of the cake. In all the years that I had lived in New York I had never, ever watched a hungry man eat.

I was ashamed. He made me ashamed that there were hungry men. Ashamed that I had never been hungry and could not even conceive of what this little boy was feeling.

So all I could say was *I'm happy you like it.* I smiled at him.

Well, sir, I's awfully happy you think so.

Do you have friends? I asked.

Hell no, they'd jes steal what I steal. Dawg eats the dawg as they says in the jukes.

Washington, are you alone most of the time?

Mos.

Where were you born?

Born in Alabama. A dirt farm, Mama tol me. She born eight children. Six die already.

That's you and one more. Who else is there?

Sister, he whispered, and started to eat more cake, the crumbs rolling down his chin, his *gaze shuttered. Sister who makes her money selling her body round somewhere. Ain't seen her fo about a month or mo. Mama don't want nothing mo to do with her. Says she be a sinner.*

And what do you think?

Oh, I suppose I love her all the same. What's the difference 'tween what she do and what I do? Stealing is stealing. I figure I ain't no more likely to go to heaven than Sister.

And school. Did you ever go to school?

He licked the spoon until it was silver again, one side and then the other, then shoved it back into his pocket. *Now where would I go to school?*

I saw you reading the newspaper on the corner this morning. You can read.

I can. Pretty good too, I can read enough to know the world ain't right. I picked it up and, well, I knows the Bible real good.

He didn't look at me when he said the word Bible, but smiled as though he knew a great secret. I noticed that his large head was matted with greasy substance, little balls curled inward, turned at an angle that shut me from his life. He wiped his mouth on his naked arm, closed the cake box, retied the string and said: *We come fo the job that ain't. The union problems suppose to let the blackies get the job. But we get killed with the knives. White man comes down the street yelling 'black man come to work. We gots work fo you. Fifteen cents a day! Sign up! Sign up!' I tell ya, I ain't stupid. Ain't no yella dawg!*

The thought of this made me angry. I felt tears releasing on my cheeks. How could we let this happen? I sighed and could find no words to say but *I'm sorry*.

Well, mista, he snickered, *we went from being darkies to blackies to niggers. Wat ya think's coming next?* He reached into his back pocket and brought out a part of a torn newspaper that was browned by age. He unfolded it and shoved it at me. *Here's the big news*: **SECOND INVISIBLE EMPIRE RISES IN ALABAMA**.

Where is your mother, I asked, handing him the cake box.

Ya really wants ta see?

I nodded.

He took me to the place where he lived with his mother. It was the corner of a basement in a tenement three blocks from Delancey Street. We walked along an alley that was spattered with black coal muck. Shadows danced on the crusty brick walls, but no light emanated in or out of this strange world. I saw no street signs to mark our way. I only knew we were near the Jewish district, because I heard the noises of the busy day blasting like a thousand chattering tongues. What was to become of the languages of these streets? And the smells were comforting; onions and beans and meats and sweets, a place not to go to in hunger. How can Washington stand this daily assault? He carried his box under his left arm, his head high and rigid, as though he had been given charge of the Pharaoh's heart. It was I who trembled at the thought of it all.

You're bringing me to a place I've never been, I whispered.

He turned and smiled at me. *We all be strangers in many strange lands. Amos wandered mos a his life and wat da ya tink he found?*

I don't know, I said.

Den I suggest ya read ya Bible one day.

69

Elijah Rising

He stopped in front of a three-story building, the paint had long faded, if it had ever been painted at all. On the first floor, the windows were covered with newspapers and brown sacks.

The Finklesteins own da building, said Little Washington*, and they's me and Mama stay here now. No charge, says Mr. Fink. Mama used to wash their clothes and now he jes let us be. Dey bring us funny, salty food sometimes. Mosly fish. Mama likes it.*

Are you still hungry? I asked, because I was, I was hungry but too embarrassed to let Washington know that. A world of guilt here as it was anywhere else in the world.

I don't gets hongry much, he said, his chin cutting the air. *Mama say my stomach's no bigger'n a sparrow's.*

In the distance, I saw a low fire. The smell of acid and burning rubber sickened me. *Why are they building fires in this oppressive heat?*

They's cooking rats, said Washington.

Pooled water vapors rose hot from the crevices of the cobbled path. Garbage was piled against the buildings, creating a wide, yet dark tunnel. Not even a merciful rain could wash away the squalor, much less the absent municipal workers. Had we abandoned the public good so soon?

I followed Washington through a hanging door and down five cold steps and into a cellar. He pointed to a bed.

She was indistinguishable from the brown dirty rags that were piled on top of her body. A sour smell drifted toward us as we stepped further into the room and moved toward the bed. Dirty air pushed into my lungs and I wrapped my right hand around my nose and mouth. I cannot say that her eyes were weary; she was beyond that. They were darkened pools of exquisite pain, endless, bottomless time reflecting images that stared at me. Her skin was pulled and dried on her skull and face, the ancient mask of her ancestors, like photographs I once saw of the shrunken heads from the deepest, darkest places of Africa. It was an archaeological text on Africa considering the falsity of curses. I am not so sure now. Her lips were pulled tightly up to her nose like the sneer from my Mother when she had pretended to kiss me goodnight. I am surprised there were teeth in her gentle head, and they were there all white and opaque like precious pearls set delicately in a hallowed shell.

What is my Mother doing then? Was she at a club lunch, a garden tea, or, God may save her soul, a charity event, where she was surely wearing her skirts pulled up just so to avoid the ground upon which she walked. Mother's bedroom, which I had been permitted entrance only a few times, at least that I remember, vaulted over twenty feet high. A chandelier sparkled, a gift from Mr. J.P. Morgan, under which she consumed breakfast and early tea propped up in bed, always dressed in pink or soft blue. She was better suited for Prussian blue. I was allowed, a shy boy in short pants that itched my crotch, five minutes with her in the morning. I was not allowed to touch a thing.

Washington's Mama made no sound, no gurgle, no groan. Near the head of the bed was an egg-blue bowl where red and yellow sticky soup quivered. I gagged and turned away, suppressing the bile that involuntarily came up my throat. It was the smell of sour death.

It's the consumption in that bowl, he whispered.

Has she been seen by a physician? I asked.

No money fo that. Wouldn't come out here anyways. The city stopped sending out to the po.

I can find someone. A nurse, perhaps, I said. I gathered my courage and turned back to stare into his mother's eyes. She did not blink and I knew she was dead. There was a shaft of light moving slowly into the room from a small hole near the top of the far wall. I gauged that it was the opening near the street and I heard a man and woman laugh. This slit in time would never be a windowsill used by robins, from it the swoosh of the ocean would not fill the room with the sweetest sound I knew, the smell of fresh

peppers and strawberries would never float through to make these people hungry, and a young brown girl would never touch another hand with love.

A shabby Bible rested on a chair near the far wall. The light shone on it. Washington lifted it up and I noticed for the first time that his hands were large, his fingers long and delicate. Was he only ten? He pulled the chair next to the bed, pushed the putrid bowl away with his foot, and sat. He opened the book slowly, smoothing the page with his left hand that was all long and bony, dirty brown with soft pink padded

fingernails. He began to read and his voice was deep and smooth, clear and strong, haunting, and, yes, melancholy. I had longed for that voice all of my life . . . *and there came two angels to Sodom*, he said.

Elijah Rising

Dust and blue smoke danced and twirled in the lengthening slight beam of light that seemed to caress his mother's chest. I had not prayed since I was a child. *Ease the burden. . . . and they smote the men that were at the door.*

I went over to Washington and placed my hand on his shoulder, for I knew of nothing else to do to comfort him. *Washington, you must know that she is dead*, I said. I felt all bone and pain under my hand.

I know. I's praying 'til I can find a place to lie her down fo good.

Let me help.

She sho would've liked that cake, he sighed, looking up and into my face. The whites of his eyes were like bright mustard, his large mouth encased with dry blood at the edges. I do not remember him ever really smiling.

I left him with a promise to return.

I used to wake between clean, white, fresh sheets that smelled like lilacs, and be served white, foamy warm milk in Mother's pink and blue flowery cups that were allowed use only for special occasions. And cinnamon rolls, a soft-boiled egg, flat toast. But now my mornings were occupied with an empty stomach that lasted until ten o'clock. I would not allow myself food until then, and a cup of coffee and a chunk of bread was my first sustenance. Sometimes I bought a cold boiled egg, but more often settled for pickles.

That morning the air was good, the streets were churning already, and the yeasty smell of baking bread finally let me be hungry. I bought a chunk of bread and black coffee from Mentel's Barkery. A young girl with spreading black hair and olive skin smiled at me as she handed me my purchase. Her lips were full and pink. I knew her name was Rachel. She was Herr Mentel's daughter and spoke no English. I ate as though I had died and come back to life, as though food was all that was worth living for. For some, there really was nothing else some days. Then I bought a peach and was satisfied.

On a street corner an old lady was selling flowers; gladiolas and daises and green sprigs. I wanted blue flowers for Washington's Mama, but I could not for the life of me conjure up the image of blue flowers.

Lyn LeJeune

There must be blue flowers. *Flowers fer your loved one*! she yelled, even though no one was around . As I remember, the old lady was always dressed the same; long brown dress, a gray shawl, men's black boots, and I wondered where and if she ever changed her clothes. She smelled like dead fish. *Flowers fer a yer gurl, honey*? she asked me. I studied the flowers, wondering which I should buy. *What one's good for a funeral*? I asked her. *Daises would be a proper one, sir.* So I bought a bunch of daises.

I had made a promise I couldn't keep. Washington's mother was buried in the Negro cemetery, without ceremony or benefit of spiritual blessing, in a field, a piece of land where broken, hungry dogs rummaged and howled night and day. The city authorities had discovered the fact of her death from the Finkelsteins, and the body had been removed early in the morning, while I ate my bread and felt the smooth, black coffee rush down my throat. If I had hurried, perhaps I could have convinced the workman to allow her a fitting removal and a train-ride to her home in Alabama, as I had promised Washington. But, she was rudely taken, placed on a wagon that usually hauls garbage, and Washington walked away in the opposite direction of the rumbling wagon that held his mother. The young boy who told me what he had seen held out his hand and I gave him a nickel. No, he said, he had no idea where Washington had gone. *What good is guilt*? I asked him. He laughed and ran away.

Dogs and more dogs littered the land that housed the final place for the dispossessed. This place had no posted name, but it should have been the Place of Innocence and Poverty. How can the hungry make crime? They were buried without mercy, born without being called. I had read in the *Times* that rabies was a concern of the New York Board of Health, so I walked quickly along a single path and toward a wagon and two men whose forms created an eerie picture of hell.

Do you know where an old woman has just been buried? I asked them. *Old women everywhere here, fella. Gota name?* the tallest one said. I was no more than three feet from him and could smell his rancid breath. His face was as red as his hair and I was sure he was drunk. How else could he get through the days with gravedigging as his profession? He sneered at me, showing black teeth, like rotten kernels of corn. *It's an old Negro woman. You took her from near Delancey*, I said. *Ole nigger she be, eh? Over yonder, by that branch. She sure did stank up the wagon,*

73

laughed the little one. I noticed that his pants were wet in the front and the rankest odor of urine touched my tongue. I pressed my lips together and walked away. The shushing sound of shovel to dirt followed me.

The earth covered her grave like the rags that had covered her dying. I heard laughter and turned to see the gravediggers watching me. How deep had they bothered to dig her grave so that the dogs could not reach her? Had Washington's mother been at least capable of seeing her life as an illusion, so that she measured her pain only by the constant rhythm of her son's reading from a worn, Hebrew Bible? If, at the end, she had seen good memories before her, I hoped that she had drowned in them. I placed the daises on the grave, not knowing where her head rested, for there were no grave markers there.

I wandered around the slums for days and could not find him. I inquired about his sister, walked through the worse parts of town where Negro prostitutes worked, and checked in with the people at the Russell Sage Foundation in Harlem. All the while his face lingered before me. I had to find Washington. Oh, for many reasons. I think I had found an object of my desire and I knew that I had to write about his life. God forgive my weaknesses or was this all just my simple nature? He was nowhere. Gone. Children like Washington never registered for anything; not school, not jobs, so there was no way to trace his whereabouts. I simply had to roam the slums.

The people all over the slums and really all of New York were scared. The government had called a quarantine of the entire tenement areas only. As though things weren't bad enough what with the other slum diseases that the Board of Health had to deal with. Like diphtheria and scarlet fever and tuberculosis. They killed the children first. Ships had to come into the harbors to bring supplies, so a quarantine would leave the city totally bereft. They only stopped the ships for smallpox and typhus and cholera. *Get your lime ready*, announced fliers. And to make things worse came the belated news that Joyce Kilmer was dead. He had been killed on the Western Front, a statistic of the great Battle of the Marne. He died, . . . *as foolish as winds that blow against a star.*

Lyn LeJeune

Finally Indian summer bathed Central Park in sparkling colors. The bright sunshine was like reason in a crazy world. Yet everything was nothing but contradictions. I went to Foley Square to attend the second trial for *The Masses*. Max Eastman and most other writers had been charged with violating the Espionage Act. Jack Reed was back from Russia. He looked worn out, his face gray and shrunken, but he was, as I had always seen him, both in person and photos, smiling, ever smiling. Edna St. Vincent Millay was also there. I'd read that the writers could go to jail for twenty years!

After five days of silliness (how else can I describe something that makes no sense), they were all set free, because the jury could not come to a unanimous conclusion. But all was not well for the socialists, and Reed gave a talk at the Club pointing out that Debs just got sentenced to ten years and the Wobblies were all but destroyed. *No*, he yelled, *this is no victory, the fight must go on and on and on!* I looked at him and knew he would be off to Russia again.

I had decided to continue my stories and wait on the one about Washington. Sadly, the young woman's typing business was a bust, and she had entered the shirt factory (Yes, the one that was to burn and killed so many young women!). So, I had a good reason to indulge and buy a typewriter, although this machine did not make the words flow any faster. But I was told that I could only have my work considered for publication if it was in typewriter form.

Samuel: He speaks a language that is not the language of his country but his faith. He is Hasidim, a young Jew who studies his books to the exclusion of play and open air. His hair is almost white, straight, and so different from the other boys with whom he walks to school. He is already bent, like an old man whose bones can no longer hold his weight. The tassels of his shawl quiver as he plods forward. He watches the ground and not the world. Except that one moment when he glanced sideways, when the sharp notes of a piano drifted down from a music studio. His eyes, bluer than quartz, large and round and excited, were surely fashioned by the hands of God and set perfectly into a tiny white face. The mouth was copied from the portrait of

Elijah Rising

God's favorite angel, so pure and pink, quietly curled in a smile that could never be broken.

Before I finished Samuel, I caught the influenza. My stomach had turned inside out and I was feverish and weak. My hands trembled when I tried to lift the razor to my face. My eyes were bloodshot and puffy, a pink rash had cropped up on both of my cheeks; my skin dried and cracked so that my face looked like a map of an arid plain. I swayed and grabbed onto the rusted sink. After minutes of this, I'd steady myself and manage to shave, although I drew blood that dribbled down my chin. I tried to leave my lonely room. But I was in a delirium, my pulse crashed in my ears, fast then slow. I remember laughing, looking for keys in my pocket, because there were no locks on the door. What's to steal, eh Washington? I lost weeks of my life. Ghosts appeared like jabbering apparitions. I knew a high fever could damage my brain. It was as though I were falling down a deep shaft, like *Alice in the Wonderland*. And there I met a tall old man, thin almost to emaciation, clad in supple gray clothes. As he leaned towards me, he nodded and reached for me with hands that were orange claws, then he stuck a talon in my ear. I was shaken by heat. His yellow eyes laughed, he spread his wings and flew out of a red door. I was then left in an austere room that had been stripped of the gilded trappings of the last century. I had become part of the modern age, not gaudy or rose-colored, but moving and rolling toward me like thunder and tanks. Glass and steel surrounded me and I thought I was in the Equitable Trust Building. I was confused and my stomach lurched and then I vomited. I thought I had come to Mother, that this was her house. The ceilings were high on high and the many windows projected bright light like a motion picture.

There was a telephone and piped in heat, hissing and blowing steam, and there in a corner was an icebox full of rye and rye and more rye. I remember being cold and hot at the same time, sweat poured from my forehead, shivers trickled down the small of my back.

I woke up in the morning, and to this day I don't know which morning. Time had passed and I had lived through this thing. I stumbled to the window and leaned out. Men and boys and girls were running up toward downtown. Several women were standing in a group and I could see that they were weeping. Then sirens went off and the silence in my

76

head was filled with the world again. Someone yelled: *The war is over; thank the Lord above, the war is over*. I wept at the eleventh hour of the eleventh day of the eleventh month.

Yes, my recovery from the influenza was long and painful, but I was one of the lucky ones to survive. The papers had been full of news of the dead; death in war and now by the hands of an unknown foe. No one knew where this plague had come from and the authorities would not conjecture when it would leave us. In one month eight hundred and fifty one people had died in the city. These numbers were greater than the daily war counts. Talk was that maybe two hundred thousand Americans had died, not on foreign soil, but on our own soil. Had God spoken and we were not listening? I believed that God had been talking to us for years. We just didn't listen. Retribution is retribution.

All I had to say was that word, retribution, and the image of Little Washington popped into my mind. I read every newspaper I could get my hands on, but I knew that the papers would not bother to mention a small Negro boy even if he were found. *Unidentified, unidentified and unknown,* kept going through my head.

I had heard nothing from the magazines about my stories. At least the world could look forward to a winter without war. Wilson was in Europe bringing peace. He reached the shores to cheering crowds; they thought he was their savior. But what man could turn back the hands of time? And another poet is dead, killed at the edge of the peace that he could not know was coming to save him. Good-bye Wilfred Owen. *But the old man would not go, but slew his son; And half the seed of Europe, one by one.*

Depressed by all the news, I went to the Society for the Poor to make my donations for the children, one in particular, the St. Joseph's Orphan Asylum that had moved to Pleasantville, New York. I moved my fingers along the list of children's names until I stopped at the name *Helen*. The trains were crowded with children and families and rushing soldiers. The war had been over for weeks, and the young men returning home were buoyant. That Christmas and New Years at least promised them some kind of future. I went home to write about Helen.

She is a child that bears the shame of a clubfoot. In the snow, her long drawn-out footsteps mark her path, so much

Elijah Rising

like a life that had been dragged out from her mother's womb into the world. Red, thinning hair springs from her head in clumps, grease adding a glow that looks like new blood. The first time she begged for pennies, she held both hands toward the passing humanity. Hours went by before she had a weight and substance for her pockets. Then the light snow came and she appeared gloved and shod, with a long brown coat that had been cut near her ankles to accommodate her small form. That day she did not have her hands filled; perhaps she looked too warm, not desperate enough, not close to death. There are miracles in this world, and Helen is one. For she survived twelve winters on the corners of the city and was finally rescued by a woman who needed extra maids, had seen Helen during a society fund-raiser tour through the worst parts of New York, and thought her demeanor submissive. Helen will marry her kind, have too many children who will at least bring her joy in their early years, become an old lady at the age of thirty, and again find her place on the streets. For in this life we seldom see two miracles touch the same life.

The trains continued to roll into the city, thunder shattering the still, cold air of winter, one after the other, delivering the soldiers who are alive; but I see from their eyes that they are no longer whole. I remember the day that I'd watched them happy and forward looking, as though war were simply a great adventure, a trial that would prove their manhood. They were kissed then, their hearts afire with young love for the girls they would leave behind. Mothers and children and fathers pretended that pride soothed the anticipation of death. How could they have known, any of them, that death waited, laughing, his hand stretched out, protruding from the still, black shroud? I think they knew, the boys. Men know death, women see life first and hope for the better part of what we are. Then, it was like summer, where in New York we can still hear the birds' song above the honking of the automobile. Flowers were thrown and caught and gathered up by young girls to sell on the streets. It was not summer now; the cold froze smiles that were fake, that were enveloped in fear. The smiles of the women were smiles of relief and supreme worry not knowing how they would sleep next to these men and listen to their screaming dreams. They knew that their lives would never be as before everything fell apart.

I went downtown for my books and there was still so much talk of war. But I purchased what had been considered by many to be the most significant novel of the year 1917. Where had I been to not pick up this book before? I supposed it was now out because it is dedicated to the life of Rupert Brooke. It was St. John Ervine's *Changing Winds*. I read it quickly, in one sitting, while I sipped the rest of the beer I had stashed under my bed. This is not a book to savor, but to finish and get on with life. It was all about internal war, internal Ireland, unending, brutal, a place from which we must sail or perish. Hadn't we had enough yet?

WHAT THE TALKERS WERE TALKING

I have heard what the talkers were talking, the talk of the beginning and the end,
But I do not talk of the beginning of the end.
—Walt Whitman

Elijah Rising

I read the most amazing article one day. An expedition from the American Museum of Natural History had found a lost Indian tribe right here in the U.S. of A., Arizona. The first photos were in the newspapers for the world to see. None of these people looked particularly happy to be found. They were called the Havasupais and lived at the bottom of the Grand Canyon where the trickle of water fed their sparse crops. I had to inspect the faces of these people, their deep-set eyes that looked at the outside world with hidden trepidation I saw it in the face of the old man who knew that he was better off without us, better off to have remained lost and away from a civilization that has just allowed the killing of millions of people. The Havasupais had been discovered and were truly lost. Would Sargon come back to take them away, the eleventh tribe, back to the kingdom of Israel?

I posed a question for myself and for the times. Where will all the new scientific theories bring us? And yes, I still looked for Little Washington, still held my pen, waiting.

Mister Theodore Roosevelt was dead. So there is a sign of the passing of our time. Right when the boys are still marching down Fifth Avenue, straight home to mother. But Quentin will not be there, not little rugged Quentin who was sent off to war by bully daddy. Poor Mister Roosevelt. It was not that I did not feel very sorry for his last years. I did admire his spirit. He was a memory for me, a childhood vision that I followed through the years. I think it was at Sagamore that I first laid eyes on him. He held me on his knee and bounced and bounced so that it was all I could do not to spew my lunch. Father was so proud that he had been invited. A short fat man is what I remembered, with big yellow teeth and magnified eyes. He was a scary image to me, so that I can still feel the relief in my chest as he let me off his lap. *Now son*, Father said, *tell Mister Roosevelt thank you.* I nodded and ran off with Quentin. Well, years later the flaming Progressive was not Father or Mother's favorite man. The constant example of the man as righteous and brave and true and the duty, duty, duty that beat in my head was silenced once he started busting those trusts. What would it have been like, this country, before the war, if they had understood his intentions and not been taken by the spell of the Hill? Were we less or more without you, Mister Roosevelt? Was there a purpose to the words in your chest deflecting that bullet, so that you were not yet ready to fall on the sword? But the country turned its back on you and there's the shame. Another lesson: What people shall blindly follow a perceived redeemer?

Winter was again a trial. At least the coal and gas were better supplied, but only for those who can pay. I read in an old copy of the *World*, old because we were again passing papers around for fuel, that a young mother went to a cemetery to decorate the grave of her baby that had died about a month previous. When she arrived at the cemetery she held a bunch of red cloth flowers, sewn by her cold hands from the baby's worn and now useless blanket. Folded over against the mean wind, she traversed the bleak earth looking for the little marker she had picked out, purchased with money begged from neighbors she barely knew. She could not find it. When she asked the whereabouts of her baby, the caretakers responded that there was no record of her baby's resting place. She returned to the funeral parlor and a search brought to dark light that the baby had not been buried, but remained bundled in a drawer awaiting the thawing of the earth. What must this sorry woman see before her eyes when she falls to bed at night? She cries out against the hunger screams of the children in other rooms. I heard them myself and was ashamed.

And then the rich were throwing parties for *little unfortunates* on the ships of war like the *U.S.S. New York*. Al Smith was governor.

One dark evening I thought I saw him. Again a small dark figure scurrying along an alley. I ran after it, rounded a corner and the alley ended. It was not Washington. It was a tiny black girl with eyes that could break the heart of the most callous monster.

Hannah: She is black and she is night, with round eyes whose whites glare out her soul. She stands outside the Metropolitan Baptist Church, which is now so society-like. Purchased and paid for on 7th and 128th, it is a model of the lengthening Negro quarters of Harlem. She cannot go in. She is not dressed for it. And the people file in one by one and two by two. Fur coats purchased fair and square from the houses of dead animals. And jewelry; oh, yes, green glints and sapphires they say, when the names were used for the ladies and not the jewels. And Hannah stands back behind the corner of the building and watches and dreams the dreams of young girls. She wonders, her eyes full of tears of joy, if there are black princesses and princes and whether she can be saved if she only had the right shoes. But her sisters, step or not, do not come anymore. They have disappeared into the night, walked away from her with no mama or daddy.

Then Hannah hears laughter like chimes in the air, and snowflakes are falling on a pretty lady. Her lips are so red, her teeth are so white, that Hannah cannot believe that she is real. A man in a black robe stretches his arm to the pretty lady and Hannah hears him call her by name. Valerie. Valerie is like a song she hears coming out of the doorways at night, when the low moaning of the trumpets and saxophones plays with the cold. She wants to go in with them, be part of the clapping and swinging and singing. But her clothes are not fit, she is not part of them, she is alien, alone, blacker than the Negro. Invisible to her race even here. Now. But Hannah can sing. She sings unlike anyone before. She squats in the alleys near the clubs and hums with the horns. The first time it happened, it was like the music came out of her stomach. They say music fills a soul, but that comes from the outside. The music was born into Hannah and was just aching to come out. She hummed with the horns, closed her eyes, lying there against a molded brick wall, its cold fingers trying to break into her bones, and the song came: I don't knows when I been so broken in two. Dear Jesus, save a poor girl likes me. And the song floated into the night, note after note, skipping down the alley and up 7th Street and entered the Metropolitan Baptist Church and God heard and rejoiced for to Harlem had come hope.

Oh, hell and damnation. They were at it again, trying to make us all bone dry. Are we not sensible men who can regulate our own drink? And what of the poor sots who hang out on the streets? What will be their resort? The drinking is not the root of the problem. They'll only find something else. So, I suppose I'm off to the last chance before the double taxes take us over. Gibson rye for $23.00 a case.

Lyn LeJeune

You'd drink too if you had read this story: A young man walked into Pennsylvania Station not intending to go anywhere. He was about thirty years old, five feet three inches and estimated at one hundred and fifteen pounds. He was wearing a blue serge suit and a black or brown derby with matching overcoat. (There was some disagreement among the witnesses as to the true color of his clothes.) Yes, his shoes were probably black or dark brown. But all in all he was well dressed and clean-shaven. He looked like a presentable young gentleman. He then shouted to the crowd something like: Well, people, I had a good time in this world. I've traveled all over and now I don't have anything left. Don't think who I am or where I might come from. It is not important. Then he pulled out a silver stopwatch and looked at it. Those who glanced up at the station clock said it was three-thirty. He took a gun out of his coat pocket, put it to his head and pulled the trigger. Perhaps he was bone dry, too. The incident was the great subject of discussion at *Mac's*. There were varying opinions. *I think he came home to a family and had no money to take care of them, so there you go. Oh no*, said Mike O'Mally, *it was the war that done it. He just kept hearing the bombs go off in his head and couldn't take it anymore.* Well, Mike's rendition was easy to believe, because Mike was in the war and came back. He had lost one leg, though, and said that he was just about good for nothing. He was looking though. *Maybe them unions will help me*, he said. But Peter Pikes had the best estimation. He said that the young man was little, that's what the evidence said, *so he probably didn't even go to the war. He had been hiding like those damned pacifists all the war years. And now he comes out and people ask him how did the war go and he's got nothing to say. They keep asking and asking until he can't take it anymore. So's he ups and blows his fool head off. Yeah*, we all grumbled, raising our glasses in unison: *Here's to the guy who blew his head off. Good riddance.*

One night I dreamed about women tending roses. The roses were the color of new flowing blood. The sky was dark over their heads, rumbling. A small house stood behind my dream, maybe a little to the right. Sometimes I thought that I was having two dreams at once. Water was draining from the slate rooftops and splashing slushy onto the crooked cobblestones. The

85

roses vanished, not suddenly as what a dream is, but slowly so that I could see the colors turn from crimson to vermilion to pink and then stark white. Streams of shit and whatnot surged down the road and the scene became a city. A small-framed boy, who I knew was fourteen but could not grow because of the muck, smiled and waved to me. I didn't know where I was, I was just standing somewhere watching. He yelled to me: *The pain ain't worth it when they use young boys. My fingers are always frozen with cold and it makes it right hard to steal.*

Did I have this dream because I longed for Little Washington? Or perhaps because the day before I saw a marvelous painting. On 34th Street was a studio loft of the painter Eugene Higgins. He paints the poor and destitute of New York, and I think perhaps his paintings and my writing had much in common. I loved his *The Street Corner in Subterranae* and *At a Rotten Dive,* a painting of a boy and girl standing on a street corner. Had Eugene Higgins seen my Joshua and Madrid on the same days as I had?

I talked to a gentleman from the Health Department who stopped in at Mac's for a drink. He was a physician by training. He was not keen on the prohibition, although he did say that the drink could kill some people whose livers were not so strong. I was curious as to the leftover feelings from my bout of influenza and asked him if he thought cocaine or heroin would be helpful for brain fever spells. He told me that cocaine and heroin were the worst and there were moves to stop doctors from using them. Instead, doctors would begin using aspirin and cocaine tablets for those who could not shake heroin. *It's a vicious cycle,* he said. *The government is making preparations at North Brother's Island for addicted men, so that they can get drugs there and no other place. The war is what brought much of this on, the heroin and cocaine use.* I was astounded when he told me that he thought there were some two hundred thousand addicts in New York. No, he told me, it was not the drink that was the danger. *So prohibition will not improve the lower classes after all*, he said, and ordered another drink.

The next day a total solar eclipse darkened the earth and sent all manner of religions scurrying for answers. What did such a phenomenon portend? So I dropped in at the Thanatopsis Library and Inside Straight Poker Club. I once had a passion for playing cards. The buzz was all about the eclipse. Some said that it passed over South America and then went over Africa and that it proved Mr. Einstein's theory of relativity. *How's that*? I asked. An old gentleman with a long gray beard and tiny gold rimmed glasses

laughed and said: *deviation of light rays in a gravitational field, pulling. And what of the NC-4's first transatlantic flight*? I asked. *Should have been done long ago. Damn war put us back,* he growled.

In the morning, I woke to heat and noise. Outside of my window they were celebrating the birth of a nation. It was July 4, 1919. But there was something amiss in the land, something I saw as foul. We flew up to the heavens in ships and theories, but could still not live together in peace. Telescopes at Mount Wilson took pictures of the moon and the stars, and the Milky Way was no longer the stuff of children's dreams. The summer began with so much promise, but was turning red. In Georgia a mob tied two young Negroes to a stake and burned them alive. Fire was upon the leaves of autumn, fire upon the cross of shame. Fire everywhere; a drought of the spirit that could not be purged by water.

Who will save Little Washington?

Hannah, continued: *She has grown and her song has inflated her life. The tones and sounds assail her day and night, so that she gets no rest. And as her songs form and take flight, she has become a beauty. Little, awkward, pigeon-toed, slant-eyed Hannah sways now when she walks, she fills the sidewalk with her womanhood and sends all men who see her reeling in hot imagination. She is black and she is white and she is all things to all men. Who will capture Hannah? Make her his own, make the sparrow sing and become a black bird. Fly away, I say to you, Hannah, fly away before you are captured. But she slinks into the nightclub, takes off her tattered coat and there she is in a green glimmering gown that is taken from a garbage dump, lovingly repaired by her long-fingered hands, black topped, pink palmed and soothing. Love was in that dress and she hummed and invented a song that went with it, when she was ready to show herself and tell the world that she was the singer, the swinger, the poet of song. Jazz lived in her and without her the world could not have it. Let me into the world and I will break all lines of song. Let me into the circle and I can show you where I come from. Not hanging on a tree, not on fire in a red dirt land, but here in the lights of the clubs, in Harlem, ready for the future of the Negro. I sing for America. I take away pain and I give you blue, blue songs. My songs say this to you: Night and day, the pain grows like a broken heart. No man can take my soul from me.*

President Wilson is down. He had crisscrossed the nation appealing for peace and it just seemed that we had our hands over our ears. The children cheered, as though they were the only ones who saw beyond their reserves at a future that did not want another war. The map of Europe was reconfigured and pieces of the pie were handed out to the highest bidder, or the one more capable of exacting retribution. Wilson had not convinced America that we should take account of nations across the ocean. We had had one war too many. *The Saturday Evening Post* anticipated Wilson's death and called for a businessman for president. His left side is dead, a consequence of the years of hope.

Strike blue and green and red last night and then my heart calmed to a flutter and I could write. The gas was turned to high, so my flat was hot and competing with the fever that had come again.

Joshua, continued: *The police have set up a net of watchers around the wealthy parts of town. Gold and silver and all manners of jewels have taken wing and escaped Fifth Avenue. The thief is young and agile, born of the streets and smarter than any cop that would attempt to lay hands on him. He has accepted the beatings of those stronger than himself, turned the other cheek for information, picked up garbage as a pretense for information. You work the right places, you use the right people, you steal like them. That was the thief's motto and so invisible had he made himself that it was unlikely that he would ever be caught.*
Thus did the infamous thief named little Joshua Berkowitz become the renowned burglar of Fifth Avenue. He measured his trips, calculated his plans, and by the time he was fifteen had stolen a quarter of a million dollars. He

could not be found. He became a hero to the common man, a modern-day Robin Hood, for the rumors were that it was he who gave money to the poor, had stuffed the pockets of young children with dollars and dollars and more dollars. All manner of charity was attributed to him and they called him Scorpion. Children's games extolled him, for they all wished to be like him. Fathers prayed to meet him and supposed he'd make a great president, for none was on the horizon. Little Jason smiled at this adulation, remained solitary except for occasional visits to his mother. His father called him: that bum.

A party was given for the poor children of New York. It took place on Park Avenue. It was put on by the 71st army regiment, for now that war has ended, what else were they to do? Word spread fast through the streets. Children were told to go and great presents would be given out. But only seven thousand invitations were sent throughout the organizations that cared for the children of the city. A short while after the party started, some fourteen thousand children stormed the building where the party was taking place. The police were overwhelmed, and finally the army was called out to quell the rampaging children. There were no presents there for the children; it was all a lie, and the causes filtered down to the young, who learned early that promises made were never kept. So that's a revolution.

I heard the children talking on the corners later the next day. They were not discouraged but angry, calling the 71st *a bunch o bastards*, and *yeah, they'll get theirs one day*. They ran together, these boys. They were no older than ten, I estimated. But the anger was folded over and under who they were and it carried them away so that they would soon see that to cheat and lie was an alternative to their lives. One boy I knew ran wood alcohol for his uncle, another sold his sister for five dollars, another shuffled money for the Italian hoods.

And the Reds have finally left. The navy ship, *The Buford*, dubbed the *Red Ark*, sailed out of the port of New York filled with anarchists, Reds, criminals and other public charges. The papers said that it was unknown as to the destination of the ship. The captain's orders were

sealed. What must it be like to not know where you are going? I was
beginning to know.

I saw my Father. He always took my soul away and splayed it at
my feet. Then he steps on it. I hate him.

I had written letter after letter to Mr. Frank Munsey offering my writing
for one of his many publications. I had attached several of my children's
stories but had no reply yet. I decided to detour, because I saw a man, not
a child, that I knew would make a character for a wonderful story.

> *There is about him the smell of manhood. He is left with
> one leg, an empty space that touches nothing as he thumps
> along Lenox Avenue. The crutches that support him are
> nicked and cracked, the right pole splintered at the base.
> Should he fall windward, would he be able to right himself?
> He stops every third step and twists his head back and
> forth, his eyes narrowed, as though he were in search of
> lost territory. His breathing is heavy, for he has yet to
> conquer his new and necessary gait. His mouth is large and
> rounded and open, and white teeth protrude ever so slightly
> from his upper lip. There is a large space between the two
> center teeth that is entrancing. He will not smile again for a
> very long time. He was a big boy and he is a big man. The
> war robbed him of many things: a leg, his determination,
> his sense of worth, a job. But the war gave him many
> things: rage, a sense of injustice, honor. He is a Negro who
> fought because his country told him it was his duty. He had
> accepted that, for he knew of no other course for his life.
> He had been born and raised in the crowded humanity of
> St. Louis, hungry often, but luckier than most. A laborer
> from an early age, the railroad had given him life and paid
> substantially for his efforts. He left three children and a
> wife, all loved and cherished, and in his left coat pocket he
> carried their picture. Where were they? He had written all
> the years he had been away. Letters posted at the front, at*

quarters, and he assumed that many had not made it. At night he had imagined a bullet blowing a hole in the messenger's stomach. But surely, some had gotten through to Mabel in all these years. He must have written over a hundred.

Now he stumbles down Lenox in a place called Harlem and looks at mostly black faces passing him. They smile as though he were welcome. Well, he did take that feeling into his chest. Yes, after being dragged through hell, here he is welcome. After several blocks, the cold air nestles around his body and seems to possess him. Is he home? Will he stay here, bring his family here, when they contact him. Or should he travel on to St. Louis to search? His absent leg still sends strokes of pain to his hip and panic to his brain. Who wants me now, he asked himself. He eases himself down on a stoop, clinging to an iron rail for balance. He takes off his hat and rubs his shaved head, a consequence of the ticks and flies and sores that plagued men at the trenches.

He has gotten used to the pleasant sensation of rubbing his hand over his smooth scalp and decides that he will continue a morning ritual of cleanliness. Deep in thought, mentally finding his way in a world that is starkly unknown, he hears a song. The voice is that of a woman, but it is deep and low, a baritone just as his. He cocks his head toward the sound and listens. Sun above me, ain't in my heart . . . is repeated several times, then the piano tinkles the accompanying melody and the voice tries again. He looks toward the sound. It is slowly seeping from a brick building across the street. A high building, notes the soldier, with windows that reflect the chilled sunshine. In the window that spans the entire bottom floor is a sign: Harlem's Song Club. He pushes himself up, tucks the crutches under his arms and hobbles toward the building. He instantly takes

91

Elijah Rising

the tune in, sings it in his head, and thinks that this,
perhaps, is the place he ought to be.

I'd heard nothing about my writing. The edge of not knowing was something close to despair, so I went to Polly's Restaurant in Greenwich Town, hoping to meet some of the new writers. It was a warm place, with talk of new ideas and books and the slant of the world. The people were welcoming and I sat with my back to a wall. There was one small painting and a mirror and the tall windows allowed the constant stream of sun on the hardwood floors. I turned to the chatter here and there and could make out a thousand conversations. I had become an expert with the voices, whether I saw the source of sound or not.

The most gratifying conversation hit on Jack Reed. For months the whole of the Village had walked around in mourning, for the news was that he had been executed in Finland. Now word had come from the far side of the world that he was alive, alive and imprisoned at Abo, Finland, charged with smuggling. Poor Jack, he was indicted, set up by his own country, charged with being a radical and a thief. All were in agreement here at Polly's that the jewels and money found on him when he was arrested were a common ploy by the authorities. He had been set up. But it was good news that a hero still lives? Or do dead ones give greater cause? A young man invited me to a table that was alive with conversation and laughter. He threw his arms around my shoulder and asked my name, then just said *here is our gang, and you're welcome anytime.* His name was William Parker and he told me to call him Will. I did like the feel of his arm around my shoulder. His gang passed a bottle around under the table, so I decided to contribute to the gaiety of my new friends and bring a bottle of rye next time.

I wanted to change my appearance. Loose jackets that defied the tailor or the semblance of wealth. I bought some used clothes from the carts on Hester Street. And the young women were fascinating to me. Bright fabrics and loose smocks and sandals were the standard attire. On the one hand they made themselves formless as women, yet on the other, more equal to the challenge of the conversation. But I still detested the bob, a woman's hair denuded, and bow ties, widened pant legs like the gulf between who we were and what we must become. Knees powdered to white, a blanched nation. But I preferred the Village to Princeton.

Lyn LeJeune

I had changed.

And now I settle myself in my bed, the gas heat turned up even though most would say it is not cold. I have consumed a large chocolate bar and downed a glass of rye. On my lap I hold James's Letters. I am in for the night and look forward to going directly and magically into someone else's life. Would Will like these books when I am finished? Would it not be a fine way to approach him?

Will was nowhere to be found; I asked several of his pals, and they told me that he had gone on a trip, they believed to France. Why didn't I act fast in my enthusiasm for him? Now I have lost again. I had become obsessed now with where he was. I read the travel sections of the papers as though his name would appear on some ship. New York to Rio on the Munson Steamship. Did he go that way? Or New York to Rotterdam on the Holland-American, or perhaps he stopped at the Virgin Islands like Gaugin. Where was Will and why am I again without succor?

I had been hired. I received an offer for freelance writing from *The Dial*. The editor will let me know when my piece on the one-legged soldier, as they put it, will be published. They did send a few suggestions, one which does strike my fancy greatly. A piece on Ringlingtown.

All is gaiety in Ringlingtown. As I look back on my visit, I perceive that it is no different than my waking dreams. My toy circus has come to life, at last, so to me I have not lived in the never land of childhood. Shall I pass through this world and be better for it? Oh yes, oh yes. There is here a true community of peoples. Many have traveled across the ocean, dodged war, and brought their talents here to America. Funny faces, awe-inspiring faces, faces of the deformed and grotesque . . . all of which are entrancing to me. And America loves this circus life. What of this Lilliputian population? People crammed into an automobile that rears up on hind wheels, like a horse ready for the charge. The machine races around and around the ring and sputters to rest. And out climbs not one, not two, but ten little clowns. Was this car made by Mr. Ford? No, because it is red and yellow and green, a rainbow of colors not akin to the drab assembly-line America. I think that this

93

Elijah Rising

entertainment takes us away from where we have been and even further away from where we are going. It is a cloudy gray future that we are tumbling into, despite the future tellers of prosperity. War is behind and in front of us, say the clowns as they set afire the little cannon that is made to grow longer and longer and turns from bright green to black.

What do these gypsies know that we do not? Morris is a man/woman who was born in a place deep in Eastern Europe. He told me that he does not even know the name of his country of birth. He came to America when he was a baby and only remembers noise and smells that he came to know as shit. His mother he remembers as a dark woman with long black hair on her head and cheeks. His father was never even a thought in his brain. He woke up to life one day and then his memory started. He thinks he was about five years old and he was riding a white horse around a ring. A tall man dressed in a white outfit was yelling at him to stand straight, stand tall and then there echoed through the large dome ladies and gentlemen, the man/girl rides the great stallion Imedel. And this was Morris' story, and from then on he became the riding freak of the Ringling circus until he grew too large to convince anyone he was still a child. He is now the side show called Man/Woman, for his hair has grown long and black on his head and face, but his breasts protrude so that, dressed properly, he can delude most people, rather all the people, that he is not a man, not a woman, but anyone they want him to be.

Such was my visit to Madison Square Garden and the people of Ringlingtown. They are off to Florida for the winter. How I long to be one of them. But at least I wrote my story. There is not much difference between the circus or Greenwich Village or the city or the rest of America. All strange, all striving, all different yet the same.

94

And then I heard the voices, this time not in a whisper, but loud and clear beyond the door. I opened the door but the hallway was empty. *Here come the barbarians.*

A DANGEROUS PLACE

. . .the mob had made its superstitions official.
—H.L. Mencken

Elijah Rising

Article for *The Dial* and the local newsprint:

> *The Tent Preacher Elijah Broom has broken ranks with his master Hiram Bell.*
> *The appeal of the Little Preacher is widespread throughout the southern states.*
> *His prayers for a greater life lift the people to pronounced hysteria, whether they are white or black.*
> *Last night, as this writer stood in awe of the immaculate happenings, several Chinamen came into the tent. Their faces were streaked with sweat, dirt matted their cheeks; dirt from the earth in which they work from daybreak into night, with picks and axes and their bare hands. These are the men who build your railroads, America. Yet before this night they were not permitted to enter the tents of God's preachers. They thank God for Elijah Broom, even though they do not understand his words, only his message, the sound of his voice, the trembling of the night air, the smell of their homeland on his breath.*
> *Our immigrants need a savior in a strange land. Protection, love, hope is what He Offers Because America has reneged on the promise. Elijah Broom is America's Second Coming, perhaps our second chance. It matters not your birth faith or the faith that you have thus far chosen. I dare you to look and listen to this man of men. Your croaking doubts will vanish. Come! Come to the waters next week in Gillian. You will be but a few miles from the mighty Mississippi.*
> *Wash away your sins. Come to the Waters!*

I had been overwhelmed with making bookings for Elijah's preaching. My articles in January lit a fire under the sinners, it seemed. They came from farm and cities and towns. For some of them, I knew he is no more than a show, a freak show, one that they could talk about to their friends. A substitute for the circus that came around none too often. These people needed entertainment. I wasn't sure, but I could swear I saw an old Princeton chum in the crowd last evening. He was dressed in a white linen suit (early fashion!) and his girl was one of those flappers I heard about. I had escaped the death of raccoons that they wrapped around their necks. The two were clapping and hollering like hungry cats. No matter. Perhaps some of their crimes would be washed away. I should have told them that prayer only wipes away sin after the deed.

I was just too curious, so I waited at the tent exit until they came out. I tipped my new straw hat at him and the girl. He stopped and jerked backward as though he had seen a phantom. *What in hell, old boy, are you doing out in the sticks*? he asked. The girl wiggled and the long strand of red beads that looped around her neck swayed back and forth over her flat chest.

I'm with Preacher Elijah Broom. Doing stories for The Dial and others. How'd you like the show?

Funniest damn thing I ever saw. The guy should be in the moving pictures. He's damn more amusing than Billy and that Garvey fella.

Kind of like a combination, I said.

You got it, buster.

That was not the last I heard of him, and I knew he would come back in some form or another to haunt me and Elijah. He was what was called an entrepreneur and had contacts all over the country. Who says that you don't have to be in the right place at the right time, or someone you know shows up at the right time and place. I didn't exactly tell Elijah about Robert; all I said was that I'd found "an ace in the hole," as he was fond of saying, and our journey was going to get interesting and productive.

Elijah was not a man of many words when he was off the stage. He looked at me and smiled, his dark eyes reflecting my twisted image, as though I had become Dorian Gray. *Then we move on*, he said, and then walked away from me and into the inky night.

I had never touched Elijah, not in all the times that I stood close enough to smell his skin. It was always like lavender and nutmeg. His breath was like sweet onions and reminded me of the sausage buns that I'd devoured on the street corners of Delancey. Elijah made me hungry, for his love, and God forgive me, forgive me, forgive me . . . wine into blood, bread into flesh, all things he is and will be make manifest to me. I wanted to run away and die. That was how the apostles must have felt with Jesus:

Elijah Rising

To love God and a man so completely, so longingly, that you gave up everything.

We had made our way into Arkansas with curious greetings from towns along the road. Our shows had made us all enough money for good food and clothes for the children. How Liza had grown in just these two months! How the young boys had grown into strong men! I had warned them never to venture into the towns without me.

The townsfolk from Pine Bluff had requested a tent meeting next month. March. Elijah wanted to start baptizing people. I was against it. He was going too far with the white crowd. They would think he was presuming too much. I heard what they said about him, the bad things, and he would not listen to the danger signals. He told me that those voices come from the devil. After all the years with priests and nuns and preachers, I still could not tell the difference between angels and devils.

I had arranged with the mayor of Gillian for an open field large enough to accommodate our living tents, wagons and the great preaching tent. When I arrived in the town, bringing only young Smith with me in the wagon, we were directed to a place about three miles south of the town. *Go to the big oak tree, the only one in the valley, and you can set up there*, I was told.

Thursday was the day, and I recall the events even today out of extreme and shaking fear. There was something about that tree that troubled me. Was it an obvious omen, or a joke perpetrated by the mayor and townspeople? Or something more? Smith was silent as we pulled up to the tree, and I sensed his apprehension. It was not until we drove back to the encampment and I headed toward Elijah's tent that Smith yelled to me: *It's a hanging tree, Mr. Michael. Ya'll gotta know it fo sho*. When I told Elijah about the tree, he laughed and said, as he always did, that *God had led us here, otherwise we wouldn't be here. Remember Michael man, only God can lead us to the Promised Land.*

What then was the connection between God and logic?

I walked around like a man hanging on to a cliff. I dangled, my legs kicking and the more I kicked, the more I knew I was brining about my own fate. I waited to fall; I wanted to fall because then I would not have to live with the consequences of my decisions. But my fears were unfounded and I thanked heaven for my stupidity. I had imagined, rather seen in my soul, as I had for years, the death of Elijah. Every time we arrived at a new town, a new state, traveled a new road, I saw death in front of us, smelled the blood of it, the cold hand of time running out. Perhaps Elijah and the God seekers yearned for eternity so that they would not have to be afraid. I had yet to place my confidence in things beyond my touch; I was a man of the modern age.

The citizens of Gillian turned out in full force; I estimated over two hundred attended. There was no dispute that I could detect about who could attend. The audience was divided into white in front, blacks in back, and one row of Chinese, which I believed was a family: a man and woman and seven children of various ages. They were dressed in clothes that spoke of their homeland; they were still dirty from working on the rails, all nine of them. They must have received special compensation from their bosses, because the clanking of the hammers to spikes continued far into the nights.

The time came and Elijah jumped on the wooden stage and skipped from right to left. His voice was bolder than usual, louder. Then winds started to howl not a minute after he had appeared. *Repent,* he yelled, *for the Lord is upon you!* The more he yelled and skipped, the louder the wind howled and the more the people moved in unison, like the pendulum of a clock, time clicking into place, faster, faster into God's providential care. *You must be a Bible-believer, you must or perish in the fires of hell! Oh, Jesus Lord, lift up the poor, the oppressed, the slaves of their own evils. Banish the drunkards and the whores, the perverse and the cursed. Come to the Lord and be baptized in the waters of his Word. As the sun rises, so shall ye live!* The middle of the tent puffed upward as though it were going to pull away from the earth. Elijah raised his fist to heaven and defied the devil to strike him dead. *Send down your lightning bolt Satan, kill me; kill one of God's divine creatures!* The sound of a great train smashed against the air and I heard someone whisper *tornado.* The crowd rumbled hidden words, then the train moved away as quickly as it had come, becoming an echo moving into the prairies. Elijah had driven the devil away from Gillian. I knew the word would spread about how the black preacher saved the town of Gillian. I would be very busy from then on. But as I watched the people settle back, I recalled a line from my old Catholic days and was later to ask Elijah: *Isn't it destiny that the Lord is with you? Yes,* he said, stroking his Mama's tattered Bible, *there is no room for free will in these times. Take it from me, Michael, one word makes a difference in convincing the crowd.*

That night, against my advisement, Elijah offered his hand as that of God and promised to baptize the citizens he had saved at sunup. I told him that I was familiar with the parable of the false prophet. *I am ordained by God,* was all he said as he turned and walked toward the stage again to bless the crowd for the evening. It was the first time since my joining him that he did not smile at me. I saw it in his eyes, in his straight demeanor, that I had become nothing but an instrument for his success.

Only the Negroes and Chinese family showed up for the dawn baptismal. I supposed that thankfulness only went so far with the Gillians. Well, Elijah baptized forty-eight grateful people, outcasts from the American dream, whose places in heaven were waiting for them. As for myself, I thought of asking Elijah if my Catholic baptismal took, or should I try again.

The baptized had brought something for the celebration of life that followed. Where these poor people had gotten such food was a mystery to me. Hoarding, stealing, growing? Wooden tables were set up under the expanding oak tree. Great plates of food were laid out. My passion for food flooded back to me and I ate fried chicken and potatoes and corn and bread and green leafy things that tasted like grass. Black and yellow together, laughing but speaking languages they had yet to understand. Their smiles showed it all. Children fell asleep in their mothers' laps, old men played checkers, women walked down to the cold creek to wash the dishes. Elijah gave the blessing after the meal was completed, his hands raised, pink palms up as though he were massaging the branches of the tree. As though he could bring all the dead back to life. *The Lord be with us,* he said, and then retired to his tent, his energy spent again. How he endured the mental and physical gyrations of his preaching I could not fathom. He ate very little, water seeming to be the substance of his life. Water from rivers and creeks and jugs and pitchers and hands of supplicating women. Mary Magdalene's black hands to the lips of the new prophet.

Gillian was a monumental achievement for Elijah. Three days later the papers were full of his words and photographs showed him jumping in the air. One local newspaper called *The Arkansian*, had the headline below Elijah's picture that read: *Negro preacher stops the whirlwind.*

And then we rested outside of Gillian before we moved on.

I often watched him sleep. I thought that I could save him by this act, like new mothers who fear the death of their babies before life had a chance. His puffy eyelids fluttered, he murmured words that I could not make out, he opened his eyes and looked at me but I knew he did not see me. No matter what happened to us in this world, Elijah, I will always remember your lips, you vanished smile. Oh yes, I knew that we were heading into a dangerous place.

In the heat of the morning, the Red River looked like fire upon the waters. We were encamped outside of Texarkana and I decided to ride down to the river's edge with Elijah. We needed to plan our journey, I told him. *The Lord guides, but he has not spoken to me about our next show,* he said. *It's my job to be your front man,* I said. We sat that Monday morning under a low hanging tree, its trunk was bent forward in supplication, a result of continued storms. It was the kind of tree that brings back memories of childhood, the kind I never had. What must it have been like to be a child in the summer of the south? To catch fireflies in jars and hide behind glowing pink bushes that flashed in the dying sunset. But it was morning then, not sunset. I will never forget his face at that moment in our lives, like I will never forget any of his faces. He had changed in the very short time I had been with him. I had speculated that it was the stress of being on the road, the heavy load of rock granite when he communicated God's message to the people. These thoughts brought shame to me almost every night. Because I believed in Elijah, but not his message. And I kept taking him apart, looking at him this way and that, until it was inevitable that I'd eventually break him apart.

How had he changed? He had aged. He was no longer little Washington, no longer young Elijah. He had turned into an old man, and that is what a prophet is supposed to be. Old. *I'm tired of the lording preacher Bell*, he whispered one night. He hung his head low, so that the morning shadows made him look like a shade come back from the dead. He was bruised. I knew that he was not talking to me. *Lording over the people. These po than po folks work the land here.* He continued, his voice finally becoming stronger, like when he preached. *Toothpick sticking in his mouth makes a man look like a devil. Flinging it from side to side. I tells you dear Jesus, he breathes raw meat. Ain't what nature 'tended it to be.*

    Who are you talking about? I asked. *The man, the man is coming,* he said.

    It was then that I told him my idea. That we should move on our own, that I would manage his crusade. *A crusade?* he asked me. *Yes, like onward Christian soldiers*, I replied. *Sure thing, Michael man, we can gather the children around us, have them follow us to the ends of the earth.* Then he kneeled toward the horizon, bowed his head, clasped his hands in front of his forehead and started to pray. *Lord, you are my dwelling place...*

    I moved away from him, wondering why he had never asked me to pray with him. I went to wait for him near the wagon, aware of the snorting horses, their ancient hooves beating at the red earth. They wanted to be away from here. I realized that great black clouds now covered the sun. *We begin our Crusade*, I whispered to the rumbling air, the tall prairie grass swished in the breeze, the chewing of locusts danced in the wind. *Bad time is coming. Dat be a hanging tree, Mr. Michael.*

    When we returned to camp, Smith was waiting for us waving a large white envelope as though he held the good news to come. *It be a letter fo' ya, Mr. Michael. A true letter wid ya name on it.*

    I took the letter and read the name blazed across the envelope in bold black script, **Michael Cooke Holt**. *Who gave you this?* I asked Smith. *A man, he come tru hera in one of dem T cars.* The combustion engine was following me into dark America.

    It was a letter from Mother and I had no idea how she had found me, except perhaps she'd hired a private detective or simply had me followed. I thought the first to be true.

Michael:

I am your mother and I have a duty to let you know, as a young man, what great struggles women have endured.

Well, you wouldn't. I know that I have been sorely neglectful of your education in this realm of the real world.

I pause here to let you know that this confessional, such as it is, is by all rights and duties, painful to me as I know it is for you at this moment. Young men never know what goes on in their mothers' hearts, and I do not know whether they should. The world is changing rapidly, gratefully, unstoppably. You must be reading for it, for I have worried that you do not understand what will happen to you if you are not.

So to it: I have sent you hither and yon all of your young life. Nannies and tutors and then to that Buckley School where you told me you were so unhappy. You should have raised your voice higher in protest and I would have paid better attention. You did not, so I left you there. I know you do not feel the passion of a son for his mother.

But I must tell you that I have used my skills for good. I refer specifically to the recent passage of the Nineteenth Amendment. I feel some guilt in ignoring you, but I still know I have done well at something. Thank God, at least my father was a liberal-minded fellow, for he gave me property which I have most effectively handled. I have had to be strong to preserve his wishes, so that what he had worked for would remain yours and mine. Without the vote, women have no control in the end and most were not as lucky as I.

So, Michael, are you on the road to understanding my position? I need your forgiveness. I am growing old fast. Doctor Mallon warns me about my heart and blood pressure. I do not want to die until you tell me that I am forgiven for giving you over to my own wants and to a greater cause. You will not remember her, but try. You were no more than ten years old. She had piercing eyes, a strong chin, and indelicate hair. I see you shaking in your boots as bent down to look into your face. She put her hand on your cheek and told you that you were a handsome boy and then admonished you of your duty to give your mother and women wide berth. Do you remember, Michael? That was Susan B. Anthony.

I admit now that I am light of heart that you did not go to war. So many young men died and that you are not one of them gladdens me. My sympathies were misplaced; I realized that when I saw the despair of so many other mothers.

I have sealed my will yesterday with Mr. Horace Sneeds, Esquire. My estate is divided solidly, that is fifty-fifty, between you, my only direct heir, and the League of Women Voters. It is irrevocable and out of the hands of your father and whatever forces pretend to exert undue influence after my death.

Your Mother
Margaret Bethune Mills Cooke Holt.

PS I have had money wired to the local bank for you.

I folded the letter into four and stuffed it in my pocket. My hands shook. I realized that when all was said and done I wished to see my mother one more time. I did not want to live like Elijah and not know the fate of someone I was supposed to love thoroughly.

I laughed out loud as I imagined Father's face when the will was read. Oh, I have often thought to describe him, his demeanor, his hugeness, his steel, cold face. The last thing he said to me was: *Call me when you want to come crawling back.* What else can a son say about that kind of father?

I went into the local bank and cashed in the entire amount of money Mother had wired. Two-thousand dollars. I put it away and filled out a loan application in order to purchase a car and a truck for our crusade. I had decided that we could no longer travel like vagabonds. We had to look like a group that was, as they said, up and up. A little class would bring in more worshippers. The more worshippers the more money for the coffers of God and the bigger we would grow. Such was my first step in selling Elijah.

Well, I suppose I was used to humiliation. I applied for purchasing the autos on the installment plan and was turned down. It seems the bank loaners knew that I was associated with Elijah. As I waited, my chair turned toward the bank window, I read A&B Bankers, Texarkana, backwards on the glass, and listened to the whispering officers in the temple of gold. What had William Jennings Bryan said? Something about being crucified on a cross of gold. I heard the words black and jumping monkey and no dice. Why fight them now, I thought. What good would it do to make trouble. Surely word would move along the edges of our wanderings. I had made plans for three revivals for the summer and I couldn't have them ruined. But, by God, I wanted to tear their faces off, throttle that little man Jenkins to an inch of his life. But I did not. I wired New York for more money, dipped into my trust fund, and swore that I would let mother know that I too had a passion for life. She who crusaded for women's suffrage must now know that I, too, crusaded for something greater. Elijah.

We moved into Texas quickly, the auto and truck making a great difference in our ability to cover territory. Our first revival out of Texarkana was successful. The little town welcomed us, although a few people left when they discovered that only Elijah was to preach. I always scheduled our meetings for Saturday nights. There is not much for the people in these little towns to do as far as entertainment. So why not get the Lord into you while watching the antics of this little Negro preacher. Elijah liked Saturday meetings, because he baptized on Sunday mornings while the sun rose just like when Jesus came up from the dead. Still, he only baptized Negroes and Chinamen, and once an Indian from the Osage tribe. He was a tall, straight man with black hair pulled into a long tail. The sides of his head, face and neck were shaved clean. He spoke English very well and told me his name of Joseph Bigheart.

We got through the three revivals with only one very sorrowful incident. The night before, as though he knew it was coming, Elijah had said that what made Jesus divine was that he did not fear those who would kill him. *And that is exactly what they did*, he had whispered in that low tone that had recently taken over his once childish voice.

Now Hiram Bell showed up at our camp. He had never worn jewelry, he'd said such trappings were the inducements of the devil. And then one morning he showed up at breakfast with an extravagant ring, the setting was shaped like a skull, the stone looked like an emerald. He talked about the evening tent meeting and how there were going to be visitors from another town, a place called Dallas, Texas.

Dallas? I asked. *That's far and away from here.*

Yep, Hiram replied. *But they gonna make a moving picture show 'bout us.*

He wanted Elijah to come with him and preach for the moving pictures.

I warned Elijah, I never trusted Bell, but Elijah wanted any avenue that would make him known to the people.

The night was warm, a breeze blew in from the flatlands and I smelled the sweet aroma of bluebells. I'd hoped we'd be across the law plain by now, heading out on our own to our next meeting. The tent was inflated with winds and people. A huge gathering where there was no water, nothing but scratched earth as though dinosaurs had already scraped away at the ground, found nothing of substance and moved on.

Five men came with a camera and five black dogs held to their sides by chains pulled around the creatures' necks. They stood at the entrance to the flowing tent, their eyes sparkling, their lips screwed up in mean smiles. I knew their purpose; it was more than making a moving picture. They were after Elijah, they were there to ground him down, make him nothing but a joke. They would not have to hang him from a tree in order to destroy him. They wanted Elijah to be afraid. But they had not reckoned with a man who was so Jesus-like that there was nothing they could do to him that would make him squirm.

As I stood and watched for any movement that would harm Elijah, I remembered an article I had recently read in an old issue of *The Times*. There was a scientist from the American Association for Advancement of Science who told the reporter that science could predetermine the sex of a creature and thus breed what he called *monster pigeons*. And he had fed a salamander cattle brains and not only did the salamander slip through fire unharmed, but had changed in size by three times. When I looked back at the men, at their instrument of recording what was happening now and thus what would happen again and again in the future, I figured they had known this scientist, had been his experiment. And thus we heralded in the modern age.

The meeting was a grand success. The crowd whooped and hollered along with Elijah and a great show was made that night.

I was relieved that Elijah had escaped the night without harm. I woke early and fried eggs and bacon and made strong coffee. I had it all ready when Elijah came out of his tent. We ate in silence until Liza came running screaming that Smith was gone.

The barbarians are upon us, said Elijah.

The meeting grounds were empty of people and strewn with garbage. Dog and people shit lay in the corners of the still blowing tent. Smith was not there; Smith was not with his pals; Smith was floating in the low running river, his head caved in and still the blood flowed east toward the rising sun. I wanted to kill Hiram Bell.

We buried Smith behind a tree where bluebells sped up the hill and the air smelled of death. Elijah had not said one word as we pulled the boy from the water and carried him to his burial ground. We sprinkled lime in his grave, pushed the dirt over him, and then sprinkled more lime. *So the dogs don' ete him,* cried Liza.

As always, there was the old Bible opened in Elijah's hands. I knew he had to read, he could not bring forth his own words. The death of Smith had made something snap in him. I was afraid that the last night had chipped away at his courage. What strength had I to take us into the wilderness? *Cursed is the ground because of you;* he whispered in a deep and enchanting voice. *In toil you shall eat of it. . . . you are dust, and to dust you shall return.*

Whether it was because of the death of Smith or not, our revival crowds had changed composition. Fewer whites and more Negroes, many more Chinese, and some whose languages were not familiar right off. Germans, Dutch, maybe a few from Denmark, a couple of Italians. What do these aliens think of Elijah and why do they come to his preaching? I asked Elijah about that, *what is it that you give them that they do not have?* He was drinking a cup of water he had just dipped from the river. He sipped, then threw the rest of the water back. *Each of them have some kind of Lord. You know that bettern' me, Michael. Confucius, Buddha, a Jesus named Martin Luther, a Pope. But their Gods cain't follow them to America yet. I'm all they have, at least for now.*

For years I had believed myself to be so informed, so aware of the world and how it worked. And here was Elijah, smarter that the whipping tail of a rattler.

I turned toward the one thing I was good for. Our funds were dwindling. Elijah's followers had little money, Bell had vanished again, the whites came only to watch, the aliens did not realize that preaching was a job, that God did not sprinkle dimes upon Elijah's head just because he knew how to invoke the proper spirit. But we were paid sometimes with ham and sacks of flour and once a bottle of whiskey which the children pinched and drank in back of the tent. I said nothing to Elijah, figuring that Mama Jones' swats were enough of a punishment.

What then is the connection between forgiveness and life?

We were to move southwest to Dallas in a week. Elijah withdrew to his tent, the children played in the river, Mama Jones cooked what we had left.

Bigheart showed up the night before we left. He was riding a dappled white and gray horse and a small boy sat behind him. He came to have his grandson baptized. I went to Elijah and told him and he said he would be out soon. He was searching for the right words to baptize an innocent child of God, *Smith is gone, God gives us another*, he said.

While we waited for Elijah, Bigheart told me about the great buffalo massacre. White men had killed hundreds, he indicated by flicking out his hands ten times. The carcasses had been left behind and the Indians got only a few sacks of meat that had not rotted in the sun. The Osaga had been moved to Oklahoma against their will. He was here because he said he saw into the future and that the Indian would not survive the westward movement of the white man. So he wanted his grandson baptized so that he could fit into the new world coming.

And then I remembered something Elijah had said not long ago. *The times are against us.* And so I said to Bigheart: *The times are against you.* He nodded his head, looked across the vast low lands, at the waving buffalo grass, the shadows that swept across the world as pink clouds

110

traveled the cyan sky as though they were being called to the firmament. Bigheart did not have to leave his native land to know that the world had changed and would change beyond imagination.

Elijah came out of his tent and Bigheart led his grandson to the river. Elijah steeped into the water and the boy followed him. Cupping his left hand and dipping in the water, Elijah then poured the drops of water on the boy's head. And he spoke:

> *Tears, idle tears, I know not what they mean,*
> *Tears from the depth of some divine despair*
> *Rise in the heart, and gather to the eyes,*
> *In looking on the happy autumn-fields,*
> *And thinking of the days that are no more.*
> *Fresh as the first beam glittering on a sail,*
> *That brings our friends up from the underworld,*
> *Sad as the last which reddens over one*
> *That sinks with all we love below the verge;*
> *So sad, so fresh, the days that are no more.*
> *Ah, sad and strange as in dark summer dawns*
> *The earliest pipe of half-awakened birds*
> *To dying ears, when unto dying eyes*
> *The casement slowly grows a glimmering square;*
> *So sad, so strange, the days that are no more.*
> *Dear as remembered kisses after death,*
> *And sweet as those by hopeless fancy feigned*
> *On lips that are for others; deep as love,*
> *Deep as first love, and wild with all regret;*
> *O Death in Life, the days that are no more!*

Bigheart shook Elijah's hand and gave him a headdress made out of feathers of the boat-tailed grackle. We watched the man and boy ride away and then I turned to Elijah. *That was Tennyson*, I said. *You just quoted a poem by Tennyson.* He licked his lips and his tongue came out like a pink instrument for piercing and said: *All things derive from another. You should know byknow, Michael, that I am a learned man far better than you ever thought. Don't underestimate me. We have much work to do.*

Elijah Rising

I turned away and thought about Father. He never demanded that I love him, only that I did my duty.

We had been camped east of Dallas near a body of water called Tawakoni for more than a week. Elijah had insisted that we stick to camps and revivals near water. *Better to baptize in what water the Lord has provided.* We decided to stay there until I could be certain that the new influenza scare was over. I feared for our children; influenza always killed the children first. Liza was becoming a young woman; I saw too many of the boys stare at her. Already we had three new babies with us and had to let some of our troupe stay behind. I think that some of the young men had long intended to leave us when we could not pay them better wages. I had tried to dissuade them, telling them that working on the railroads was just about the only job they could get, and those were more often given to the Chinamen who worked for the lowest wages.

Finally there was no news of influenza and the people I talked to in town said that the epidemic had not come to Dallas after all. I distributed notices about our revival in town, leaving some in stores when I was allowed to and tacking some on posts. I paid two boys to hand some out on the streets and asked the *Dallas Times Herald* to print an announcement. It cost three precious dollars.

I'd read that Dallas was becoming the Mecca of the southwest. I remembered Mother talking about the establishment of a Federal Reserve Bank and how Father's friend, Dr. William Worthington Samuell, had bought the city its first ambulance, expanded the hospital, and the government used Camp Dick for aviation training during the war. Dallas was home to the Southern Methodist University. I took a trolley to the university and distributed notices about our revival.

I went back downtown and walked around until I heard a low moaning voice, a song, and then the prick of a guitar and then a whining sound. On the street corner was a black man sitting on a wooden box, guitar in his hand, and he sang about Jesus and going to the Lord. He wore dark glasses and kept his head tilted toward the sky. I watched him for a time, enjoying the sound of his rough voice, the constant smile on his lips. This man, obviously blind, strikingly poor, was happy. He was using a

112

pocket-knife to slide along the strings of his guitar. I put a dollar in his box and made a mental note to ask Elijah if this man could help our revival. We could do with some uplifting music. I asked the man his name and he said; *I be Willie Johnson, dey call me Blind Willie.* I listened to his song as I made my way back to Elijah and along the dirt road heading our tents.

> *Won't somebody tell me, answer if you can!*
> *Want somebody tell me, what is the soul of a man*
> *I'm going to ask the question, answer if you can*
> *If anybody here can tell me, what is the soul of a man?*
> *I've traveled in different countries, I've traveled foreign lands*
> *I've found nobody to tell me, what is the soul of a man*
> *I saw a crowd stand talking, I came up right on time*
> *Were hearing the doctor and the lawyer, say a man ain'tnothing but his mind*
> *I read the bible often, I tries to read it right*
> *As far as I can understand, a man is more than his mind*
> *When Christ stood in the temple, the people stood amazed*
> *Was showing the doctors and the lawyers, how to raise a body from the grave*

Dallas was more city than most of the places I'd been since joining Elijah. I did not realize how much I had missed bustling humanity. The farmers who had left their lands, hung in the city and waited for the modern age to save them. No different than those who came to New York from other countries, the south, wherever someone, one day, promised them a better life, or when fate took their heritage away. Had it been only a year since I had left New York? That is were I had left the voices. Why could I not hear the ones that Elijah listened to, that guided him? Where were my guiding voices? But for my love of Elijah, I was still a lonely man.

Later in the day, I passed by a large mining camp and stopped. The streets were muddy, the men all had beards and snickered, showing yellow, rotting teeth. I was sure it was a place of fomenting diseases. But I had to get notice of Elijah's coming, so I went about with my handkerchief around my face, always pretending a coming sneeze. This was a perfect place for tuberculosis. Like the tenements of New York, no worse, no better.

The miners, the immigrants, the farmers . . . all the people that Elijah spoke to, those who he wished to lead into heaven, probably could not read a word of his sermon should it be written down. My articles were read not by the common crowd, but the commentators, the social cynics, the politicians. Yes, this whole Crusade was all politic and it was a fact I had to hide from Elijah. It was the spoken word, not the written sentences, that would move the masses. And I wondered what had become of the moving picture Bell and his henchman had taken of Elijah.

I don't know what did it, but we had a full house that night. People arrived in cars and wagons and riding horses, and the miners came in trucks. The Chinamen walked. Maybe it was the drink that they hid under their pillows, or that the bosses handed out to make the men work harder, or the shame of their continuing use of prostitutes. Whatever it was, we made a fine purse.

I decided to continue to use Jesus' techniques sketched out in the best selling book that insisted that Jesus was the first businessman. Give the people what they want . . . nay convince them of what they need. In Elijah, they saw a chance for redemption. Sin is forgiven, over and over and over again even before it happens.

After the big meeting, I saw Elijah continue to change right before my eyes. Perhaps he was divine, perhaps the Lord did walk with him after all. I longed to be sure of that. Last night he came to my tent. His shoulders sagged like he carried the weight of his flock. Had it all become too heavy for him at last. Was Elijah breaking?

Pray with me Michael man, he said. *You're in great danger. How?* I asked him. *You are becoming like the moneychangers in the temple. Yes, it seems so*, I said. *But how else can I keep your crusade going? Prayers will keep it going*, he told me. *Kneel here with me.*

I did, even though I had spent my childhood kneeling in front of the priests and nothing had come of it. But it was different with Elijah. He was real, and flesh and blood and suddenly smelled of acorns and then nutmeg. Always the aroma of nutmeg. *You must believe in the word of Jesus without question*, he said. *How do I know the word?* I asked. *Everything in the Bible is true. Jesus will arise for a second time and redeem us. When?* I asked. *When you learn to suffer like Job. Then it is not bread and wine and love, the body and blood of Christ?*? I asked. *No. It is suffering that will transform our world.*

It began to snow. The snow fell hard and fast as though the sky had been severed by a golden sword. From east to west the earth was white within minutes, it piled up against tree trunks, covered the still producing berry bushes. The children rushed about in bare feet flinging handfuls of snow into the air. *But Elijah,* I cried, *when will the world have enough of suffering? How long can we endure?*

I woke beyond dawn and our camp was empty except for Mama Jones. She was washing Elijah's white shirt in a bucket. Her hands plunged and twisted the shirt, plunged and twisted the shirt as she sang: *I'm looking now across the river where my faith will end in sight. There's just a few more days to labor, then I will take my heavenly flight.*

I drove back to Dallas. After the praying with Elijah, the old sense of doom came back into my soul. I thought I would find happiness, that he would help make the ghosts go away, but it seemed that he poured more into me. So, I ran to the city as though I longed for New York. This was no New York. It was scary and desolate. I longed for home and was damned surprised at this new emotion. Even from Memphis to here we had moved a world away in the same America.

If Prohibition was the law of the land, it was ignored outright in Texas. Whiskey was just about poured into your hand if you held it out long enough. It was like I had met an old friend again. I drank until my heart was full and content, smooth and burning sucrose moving down my throat. How I had missed that sensation!

On the corner of a dingy street, I again heard the singing of the black man. This time the music of an accordion massaged the tune. I stumbled toward him and then sat next to him, feeling the wet mud seeping through my pants. I didn't care. *Sweet, sweet Jesus, bring me home. Sing, sing louder,* I told him him. *You lost in the desert again.* All I remember was emptying one of my pockets into his hat, looking into his face and into clouded, white eyes of a man that saw straight through me with his music. *I'm Blind*

Willie, I'm blind Willie, he said. *I'm blind, too,* I said. *Then you need great care, man, great loving care. Sweet, Jesus, give this lost man care.*

Elijah Rising

Last night's revival was dismal. No more than thirty people showed up. But Elijah was more animated than ever. Frenzied. The louder he called out to sinners to come to God and Jesus, the more be believed people would hear and come. His passion was disturbing, like he was losing himself, losing Washington to Elijah was one thing, but to lose Elijah to . . . what? was frightening. Was he giving over to his voices just as I had? Mine had not killed me yet and I kept them at bay by honoring someone but myself. But Elijah, Elijah was heading down the road where the hanging tree waited, for I saw it in the eyes of the people who attended his ecstasies. He brought their shortcoming home, he blamed them for their misery. Soon, they were going to still his voice. And then mine would start up again.

Texas was surely not our Arcady?

We are encamped between two creeks that rushed down toward us from mountains like a speeding train. I told Elijah last night that the sound reminded me of the beating heart of an entire nation. One that thumps so fast it's almost the call of death. He shook his head yes, yes, as I spoke. His eyes had grown yellow, the whites hidden behind a golden veil, his heavy lids like the curtains closing after a Shakespearean tragedy. *Mr. Randolph once said life is like a great black train*, he whispered, the words floating from him, *the farther the train goes, the closer we get to our destination. Did you meet Mr. Randolph?* I asked him. *Mr. Randolph is a fine man, cut out from the Lord's red cloth. Don' need to meet him to know him.*

He stayed with me for hours. I knew that he'd sensed my growing need for his company, that I had come to the realization that he would never be mine altogether, that he would never give himself over to anyone except his Lord. But he had become my reason for walking through this world. *Each man must find his own way, Michael man. If you feel alone, it is because you have not accepted Jesus in your heart. He has always called you. In your old church, in your mother's arms, in the streets of New York, on the train, and here with me. You decide what is most important.*

When I suffer like Job, I snorted.

No, he replied, *when you suffer like you do now.*

Elijah's next sermon took place in the valley at twilight. Blue and white flowers dangled on long green stalks of Indian grass. Every so often

I could swear that they were making the slight sound of bells calling us to a sermon somewhere out in the vast wasteland. They said that in Texas the rains would come hard and fast next spring. The cool breeze caressed the crowd; over two hundred from several surrounding towns. Farmers and railroad workers and miners and cowboys and prostitutes. All colors, all people of America had converged in this valley. The years had not been kind to these people. Drought, poor harvests, land grabs, railroad buyouts. Like the streets of New York I saw suffering in the faces of these people. Skinny children, pregnant women, sallow men. They were looking to Elijah for comfort. Unlikely prophet at last.

I had reminded Elijah that he would have to preach ever louder than usual to compensate with the rushing waters of the creek.

Elijah skipped across the wooden stage like a man possessed, like a man who was becoming not a man. His heels popped each time he landed, he raised his hands in a condemning gesture; then he would slide backwards as though pulled by an unseen force. Forward. Backward. Sideways. *The serpent has crawled across you land! Disease, famine, hail and wind on those who have sacrificed to false gods! Who is righteous and believes in the Lord shall be raised on the last day . . . the rapture! Follow me and be saved for the rapture! As the Lord commanded Joshua, so he commands you! Follow me! The Lord shall not forsake you. Come to the Promised Land!*

The movement of the bodies, the cacophony of the voices on a cold night, drowned out common sense. They believed. Women swooned, men ran up to the stage to be blessed. It would never end, we would go on and on until Elijah's Lord actually decided to come down.

Then Elijah stopped preaching, he stood still and, for the first time, he fell to the floor in anapoplexy of the spirit. Elijah had become divine.

The next day I sent in an article to *The Dial*. I had sent twelve so far and received good comments from the editor. I assumed they had been published.

The Baptism Between the Creeks.

In a valley between two creeks, in Texas, where farm prices have

fallen, and need and hunger has stalked the people, a phenomenon,
a miracle, is taking place. Last Sunday, over one hundred citizens
were baptized in the cool waters that flow from the cracks in the
hanging mountains. Some white, some Negro, and a few Chinamen.
I expect next week a few Germans will gather, Lutheran or not. And the man who is baptizing is no other than the Black Preacher,
Evangelizer, Elijah Broom. He has brought hope to this suffering land.
It makes a man wonder about the genealogy of David.

The next week I received a telegram from my editor. He requested that I allow release of my story on the baptismal to the wire services. The story about Elijah and the baptismal hit the pages of American papers in time for Christmas. The byline was *BLACK HOPE IN TEXAS*. My editor sent several of the articles to me; one from a Dallas paper, a Denver paper and, of course, New York. My article was quoted exactly as I had written it. When I showed Elijah, he smiled, nodded, and simply said *God's work, Michael man, you done God's work. You're doing a fine job of selling Elijah.*

SELLING ELIJAH

Many a small thing has been made large by the right kind of advertising.
—Mark Twain

Elijah Rising

I had suffered in the cold of New York, but it was nothing compared to the ice storms that galloped down the valleys of the Texas plains, to the rejection I felt when I gave Elijah his new book. *What are we doing here,* I asked Elijah last night. *It is worse than Moses' trek across God's forbidden lands.* He only laughed and shrugged his shoulders. He hung his head, as though someone were speaking to him from far away. *It is not the cold, Michael man, that cripples a man's spirit,* he whispered. Then he paused, again he listened, his head twisted toward the western horizon, as though he were being called by the trumpets of the Lord. He was, after all, Elijah. I strained to the deepening evening, hoping that I could hear just one wisp of what he heard, that somehow he could transfer some of the fullness of his soul to me. Just a wisp, I chanted inside my own unimagined soul. Echo. Echo of emptiness. I wished, at that moment, that I could die. Then this lovely man walked to me, floated on a cloud, and wrapped his gaze around me, the large, pink lips captured me and he said : *It is poverty, poverty of the soul, the mind and the body that cripples a man's spirit. Listen to America, and you will know that we are heading for a time of great poverty in all things. Listen to these people who come to us on bended knee, on swaying hips, mothers full of babies that will be hungry. Look at this land here in Texas, Michael man; it is like the desert that the tribes endured. It comes full circle, and it is God's design that we be here.*

Who are you and why am I here? I wanted to ask him. I found that at long last tears appeared on my cheeks. I kneeled in front of him, my arms around his hips, my head on his chest, and sobbed in gratitude. *I am your friend,* I screamed, *please help me*! That is all I remember saying before his hand touched my head, the big man-child hand of the New York cellar, and he caressed me like a mother does a child, unconditionally. I could kill him now and he would love me despite my evil. I had waited so long for such simple affection, for love, for Elijah to save me. Lost, lost, my innocence was lost and I was happy. Was it my imagination? Can one man save another? Make life bright and cool and sweet? Are you reading this, Elijah, some time in the future and laughing at my love? I swear it was true. I swear it on the soul of all that was true and pure and good. I swear it on the body of Smith. What do you have left after your own history? How many children had you seen die at the hands of hunger and disease? How many men given over to the black-hooded skeleton? Was your time any better than mine that you should cast away my treasure of love? Believe me, it was real and good and it was something every person who walks this earth longs for. Was it what you longed for? I at least knew what love was.

At the end of this Texas trail of sawdust and tents popping in the soulful wind, I saw him dead and me hungry again. What was this all for? I could not warm up in this life. I wanted my old voices back. They had not loved me, but they were, at least, a comfort.

We were to have a meeting that night. Because of the cold I did not expect many people. I kneeled down to examine the ground under the white tent and it was frozen. The town manager had promised to spread hay over the dirt and shit, but he had not done his job. The ground was littered with knobs of droppings from animals. How could I expect the people to listen to Elijah, and even believe him, in that filth. I could not say anything to the manager, because one harsh word would bring a ton of vengeance down on us. I had heard that the Klan had set its tentacles far and wide and had reached Texas. There in the hinterland, what Elijah always called the wilderness, it was possible to perceive the vastness of existence and cry. There were stories around that not even the worst of nightmares could blot out. I had heard the men talking in the shops, in the restaurants, everywhere I went. *Even in the hard winter we can hang 'em high.* Or*, let's let a couple of 'em freeze first and then watch what happens.* And then there was laughter all around.

For the second time I saw Elijah hanging from a persimmon tree. His body rocked with the wind and thumped against the orange fruit. Three fell to the ground and a young girl gathered them up and handed them around. A snow squall had inflated the flat plain and made unfurling waves. The sky was pink. Ten men, no twelve, congregated around the tree. Their breaths puffed out in gray clouds. Rime grew on their beards. The wind bit at them sorely. Elijah was frozen. *Now we don't have ta bury this one*, said one of the men.

I gathered the children to sweep the frozen ground and then to scatter the bales of hay in the middle of the tent. Then I had them bring water to the camp from the creek. Their tattered shoes were wrapped with old cloth. The smallest one was only four, but he had hauled buckets for an hour already and seemed not to tire. I watched him from the ragged

121

opening of my tent so that the little heat that was in there would not escape. If I die, I thought, it will be from this damnable cold.

It was all for nothing. No one showed up for the preaching. The next morning we moved on with the stark silence of winter, with the silence of the dead world. Into oblivion as the icy wind pierced our backs.

We managed to get lodgings in a small town that did most of its trade with mining companies. At least the women and children could stay warm from the iron stoves that had to be fed day and night. The boys were paid a nickel each day for gathering coal and wood.

I set about to plan our spring and summer Crusade, checking off the days until April, when I realized that it was Mother's birthday. She was fifty-five years old. How was it that when I looked at that day on the calendar that advertises tractors, that I missed her; suddenly, unbelievably, longingly, as though she were the painful thought of a person long dead. But she was not; or I thought not. I heard Elijah's' voice: Write her Michael, make peace, redeem yourself. He was a new voice inside my head, unsettling, but trying to set me free.

Dear Mother . . . My Dearest Mother . . . Mrs. Holt . . . MBCH. . .

Mother:

I have drawn a line in the cold snow: one side is yesterday, the other today. The heat from my little stove melted the white crystals, obliterating time. Where has time gone, Mother, that we have been strangers from the day I was born? Well, perhaps it is time that the past and future converge and I tell you that I did not hate you, only your neglect of my need for you. You threw me to the Jesuits, but they could not give me even one ounce of what I longed for.

They were all so academic, those priests in professors' clothing. And they were frigid, to the ends of time they will be that. They knew not how to open their souls. I wish you could know Elijah. He has opened me to love and peace and told me that the path to redemption is already here. It is I who must find it, clear the brambles, and walk without fear through the thorns.

122

Please read on Mother; do this thing for me. You must have thought that I had gone mad when I left New York. I did. Raving. I thought that a man could vanish in this world forever, without a clue, no hint, no trail left behind. Not even Mr. Holmes could detect my leaving marks. But those who seek to hide, only have to find themselves in other places; good places, bad places. They are like balls of string held tight, that come unraveled, then stretch out for miles, from one coast of America to the other. And behold, Mother, there is nothing inside.

This makes no good sense to your practical mind, does it Mother?

Happy Birthday.

Liza had grown into a young woman and I was afraid that she would be taken on the road. It was not the possibility of lynching that shadowed her every move, but man's lust. I had talked to Elijah about this and he suggested that she marry and bear children. He wanted to rename her Ruth. What was he doing now? Again I sensed that he would drive some of our camp followers away. He was harsh with the young men. His kindness seemed to leave him at times. I think he was bending from the weight of his ambitions and that we had yet to find a place for his preaching.

I worked the nearest town, and to this day cannot remember its name. We needed spring. I met a man at a bar where I was elated to find rye. I drank three glasses. The man called himself Minos and he owned the bar and several houses for alien workers. I did my dance and secured a booking. Minos guaranteed that the aliens would turn out.

We had to travel more than five miles to get to the encampment Minos told me about. Dust clouds mixed with sleet pummeled the boys riding in the back of the truck, slashes of blood ran over their faces like quick rain. When darkness fell and we were not sure how far we had gone, we all pushed into the car and trucks like a bunch of wayward, bruised clowns. We slept by the warmth of each other and woke with mouths full of sand and the cold air was gone and the flaming sun presented us with such a desolate picture that Elijah simply said *apocalypse, next I intend to see the four horsemen ride this way.* We headed out and I knew that we would soon run out of gas. Over sand dunes and barren land we went. It was as though that very night the end of the world had come and we had slept through it, wasting the last moments of our lives.

How far we goin', asked Liza. I pulled out the hand-drawn map Minos had given me and pointed to a line that went from here to there with the notation *fiver meles and ya be der.*

We already done gone five miles, chirped Liza, and she stared ahead, her shaved head trembling *with tiny bugs that chewed at her scalp.*

I stopped the car and climbed onto the hood and shielded my eyes looking four ways into the distance. I saw nothing. The wind picked up and it seemed as though a thousand sand tornadoes swooshed me up and dropped me on the ground. I was pumiced and rolled to the side of the car then all was calm and all I could hear was Mama Jones humming, humming, and her voice carried into the empty landscape *Wade in the water. Wade in the water children. Wade in the water. God's gonna trouble the water.*

Elijah stuck his head out of the car window and laughed. *We been snookered, now we gotta pretend we been thrown out of Egypt.*

On the sixth day four trucks carrying Chinamen and Indians came up over the horizon, shivering in the uptake of sandy heat. The nearer they came, the more the children clapped. The driver of the front truck was ghostly white and so skinny he looked like Lazaurus unrisen. I showed him the map and he brushed the hair away from his forehead and spit, leaving a glob on the sand that evaporated before my eyes. He said that there was nothing out where we were going, nothing but the stakes he and the aliens were laying for a railroad.

I felt like a fool. Despair hit me and then the man said: *If you all go west six more miles you all will come to a settlement called Jensen. It's really a camp for rail workers.* We negotiated for water and food and ended up paying him at least ten times the real cost of the supplies.

We waited out the end of winter, doing odd jobs, Elijah baptizing for a nickel a person, the boys hauling wood and coal, Liza and Mama Jones cleaning floors. There was a constant flow of people from many places and I was at last able to secure a booking some five miles from

Jensen. We packed up and headed out praying that soon Elijah would be blessing the spring planting. He had decided to expand his trade from preaching and baptizing to blessing. Our spirits were greatly lifted. I had to convince Elijah to buy new clothes, telling him that it was time he started putting on a good-looking show. His hair had turned white, his demeanor was one that begged for reverence. I wanted him to act straight and narrow, speaking simply because I could no longer listen to the snickering and monkey jokes and came after his performances. Back in Tennessee one local newspaper had called Elijah *Mr. Darwin's jumping black chimp* and then asked the question: *So you think he has evolved?* Didn't we at least need an air of respectability?

Ides of March. I had come to believe less in our Christian destiny and more in premonitions. I had tried to control our fate and Elijah told me to be calm, that the Lord would guide us and that we had come very far already.

We were near a place called Buffalo. Laz and the other young men were setting up the tents. It had been a horrendous morning. Some people from the town came and watched our work. They laughed at our boys and I heard one of them say that the monkey man was going to jump high tonight. I went out and worked with the boys, right along their side to show those perfidious people that I was not one of them. I hoped that they would not show up for the meeting.

That was the first time that we had trouble at a meeting. Those men came and hooted and brayed while Elijah preached. I acted courageous and like a bully and asked them to quiet down or leave. They stayed a while longer then left. Thank God. Elijah acted as though nothing had happened.

Before the sun came up, I hopped in the car and went into town to get supplies. I was handed a paper by a young woman who smiled brightly and said that I should join up to save the great nation. It was a call to join the Klan. For only ten dollars initiation fee (kleck token), I could become a member of the organization that would save America from the foreigner, the moneychangers and the savages.

For the first time there was a disagreement among our group. Most wanted to head south toward Galveston, away from the Klan, and to where more opportunities for not only jobs but also bookings could be easier to get. I agreed. But Elijah would have none of it. He wanted to head northward through Texas and then into Oklahoma. I told him about the Klan, showed him the paper, about what had happened in Tulsa. He did not want to be safe. He believed he was needed in the most troubled parts of America. *I am abiding my time until the barbarians come*, he said. I looked at him and wanted to punch him; he was endangering all of us. *They are already here*, I replied, *they don't give a damn how Christlike you are.*

His strategy had changed. He no longer waited for the formal meetings. Elijah preached on the roadside, in fields and encampments, to people who were so destitute it broke my heart. He told me that I no longer had to worry about bookings, that he would simply stop where the Lord told him. We were running out of money for supplies and he seemed never to understand or care about the economy of his Crusade.

We traveled into May and had never seen the earth in such wild abandon. The land was dry, no rain had fallen in two weeks, yet wildflowers clutched the meadows as though they were the only things that could stop the world from turning to dust. When the warm breeze flowed in ripples over the pink and yellow waves of wheat, my heart lurched. Happiness. Why could I not feel that with another human, except for Elijah? But he was growing away from me, from our group and ever more remote as the days went by.

The afternoons were hot and heavy as though a pile of new steel had fallen on us. We found a resting place under a tree that was just beginning to sprout leaves. I went out into the field alone. I had a wide view of the sloping valley below. White and tiny flowers dangled upside down from shiny green stems. I thought I heard church bells bong once then twice then echo toward me, up from the valley, skipping over the waving blue Indian grass. It suddenly felt like that very first time I walked the streets of New York: Fear because of my own inadequacy, reverence for the majesty of the city. I cannot put it down in exact words, but knew, without doubt, that I was privileged to have been there at that time, with these people, with some purpose. I had lost myself in simple reverie when a whistle pierced my solitude. The sound came from my right; where two prairie chickens were mating, their orange air sacks bloated, waiting for release.

Despite the beauty around us, those were our hardest days so far. It seemed as though we had been propelled through time. From extreme cold to heat that pickled our skin in our own sweat. None of that bothered Elijah.

One night Elijah preached to a group that had huddled along our dust-trail, their two horses exhausted and dying. They were the poorest of the poor and would take any hand offered. The low rungs on the American ladder, as one newspaper put it. I watched Elijah and feared that he had turned into a fanatic. *I am God's instrument,* yelled Elijah. *Take care of my brothers and sisters. . . Atone for your sins, eat the body of Jesus, and stay away from perversity . . . away from the evil drink and laying with whores.* I watched their faces. I don't know that they understood the fullness of his message and neither did I. But they believed and that was all that was necessary.

In June we crossed the Red River for the second time during our Crusade. The past year the swelling water frightened the lot of us and we hesitated before going across. But this summer there was a drought and the water was so low I swear we could have walked across the river. The bridges had been repaired and we chugged slowly over the rumbling planks. Liza sat near me, her face turned toward the snaking waters. I glanced over to see what entranced her. Below us, three dead cows, inflated with congealing bile, churned in the rushing water. Buzzards rode on them and pecked at their eyes. I put my arm around her and pulled her to me. *That be all there be when we die, Mr. Michael,* she shivered. *You're not a cow, Liza,* I said. *You're a person. What kind?* she asked me. *What am I?*

Elijah could have walked over the water, I think, but I know for all his praying and preaching and intents to save, he could not answer Liza's question any better than me.

I was ashamed of my negative thoughts of him. But he was getting the divine light into him ... thinking that he was God.

The Fourth of July picnic outside of Mt. Zion was so much different than the one we had spent in Texas. In Texas, the farmers came in trucks and tractors, and brought all amounts of good food. Not here. It was wagons still pulled by mules whose ribs protruded, whose heads were covered with fat black flies that drained their blood. This was the place of the depleted land, the depressed farming communities our elected officials had forgotten. Except for Mr. Bryan. I knew he was too much with the common people for the dunces of Washington. But they did not fear his campaign, because few of the people in this far out country had the opportunity to vote anyway. Really, Bryan had no hope of being president, he'd been turned down years ago, laughed at by the city moguls. The talk today was that he would be coming to town to deliver one of his famous speeches. I wanted to be there, because I saw it as an historical event and a perfect subject for an article I had been working on for over six months. I knew Elijah would benefit from hearing and seeing one of the great orators of our time.

I ate so many bowls of green leaves my stomach heaved. Collards. The outhouse was full of flies and feces and I knew I would lose what little food I had consumed if I went there. Dear God in heaven, I resorted to the bushes!

Waiting for Bryan, the entire encampment was in doldrums. The heat and the drought had brought misery and bad feelings to the land and the people; even the animals were out of sort. We were in a demented land. I thought most of all it was the constancy of the buzzards that were driving me to distraction. They lined the barbed fences from sun up to sun down. They stared and followed my movements with their eyes, like they were waiting for me to keel over and die. Waiting for a new meal. Perhaps Liza was right. The thought of those dead cows brought the sour liquid to my throat and the old sickening feeling in my stomach returned from the past. I could taste the Man-a-ce on my tongue. Fear, the pictures of the barbed trenches, the influenza, Mother, the not-so-distant past. Demented, amputated, full-blown need for divine love. Well, that was why I was there.

I sent a wire to *The Dial* to update the editors about the Crusade. It was time for me to make our mark. I had seen visions of great things for us, perhaps moving into the city where Elijah would become known or famous. But he insisted on moving further into the desert. At night wolves howled, the echoes of their baying started far away and as the night deepened the sound moved closer to us. The children cried day and night now, out of fear and hunger and still we moved on. Slowly, far too slowly.

Lyn LeJeune

But we were near the town where Mr. Bryan was to deliver the word. A Saturday, 18 July, 1923. Elijah said that he would go, that God had arranged the meeting of two like souls. Would Bryan even deign to shake Elijah's hand?

Draft article:

William Jennings Bryan. . . man, monster, saint?

On the morning of the day that he is to speak, the dirty roads leading into town are clogged and swollen with gaunt, gray people. Without smiles, they come in wagons, on foot, in old black Fords, and even on tractors. A small girl, her feet dragging along the red dirt, rides happily on a goat. Her face is porcelain white, dotted with red freckles imprinted callously by the Texas sun. Imagine, reader, that it is like the Jews gathering to meet Jesus, the call of redemption having reached their hearts years, nay centuries, before. I am told by townsfolk that Bryan brings hope to a dry land, new life to a country gone to the devil. In this part of America, a part that the East will not recognize, the world turns slowly and away from good times. For years, prices for farm products have fallen without abatement. Here, there is no jazz, no flapping, no thirst for the evil drink, and a woman's skirt still reaches to her ankles. Children wake up hungry and go to bed hungry. Ask anyone here and they will tell you the story about the farm family that had to send their nine children to the state orphanage so they would not starve. I believe it. I see it every day in the eyes of these people, and I see it clearly, undeniably, when Bryan struts onto the wooden platform. He knows from whence their fear comes, he knows how loud their hearts beat, he knows and will use their pain, laying it bare on the cross of gold.

American flags surround Bryan's stage; they pop in time with the big man's footsteps. He is tall, solid and old. There

129

is about him the smell of the common man, for he sweats and gnaws his jaw while forming the next thought, the next lightning bolt pronouncement. He has taken off his white jacket, suspenders red-and-blue-striped push against his protruding stomach. He is bald, with dust laying in small clumps on the shiny surface of his sunburned skull; or are those brown spots the marks of world-weariness? He puffs his cheeks and lets air out. At last, the gesture the crowd has been silently waiting for: he raises his right hand as though to anoint the people, he looks up to heaven, raises his left hand that clutches a black Bible, the gold embossed cross sparkles in the sun. He asks: what man will not walk across the street to save a soul, but will travel the world to prove that we are children of monkeys?

A worthy speech for the crowd who could do little to improve their own situation. I no longer feared my own ghosts. They were bright spirits compared to what we were running into. We had had no meat or milk for over a week. I had wired again for trust money. When would *The Dial* pay up? Mother did not reply to my letter, although I know it was difficult for us to get news to each other. My heart grew tender with the need of money.

Dear Mother:

I am sure the bank has notified you of my past withdrawals. It is all to good purpose and perhaps one day I will tell you the whole story. Have you received my recent letter? You may have read my articles in The Dial and The Times. The poverty and desperation here in the hinterland shames our country. Would these people have only one-third of what I had growing up? The children have legs that can barely assist their natural urge to run. What is childhood here but waiting for food, for a warm touch, for the rapid death of anyone over the age of forty? Yesterday I met a young girl who could not have been more than thirteen, her stringy hair was plastered to her sweaty face, her lips dry and cracked, with little trickles of blood at the corners of her mouth. She is with child. This baby, this dear sprite. And no, she is not married. Is this all the fault of the man who did this to her? Is it the time, the place, the fact that there are no choices here? While the cities reel from good times, the farms lay barren.

I went to hear Mr. William Jennings Bryan speak not long ago. Although I am not one hundred percent his disciple, or even ten, he did say something that struck me to the heart.

That we must walk across the street to save a soul. Mother, I am using my money for our Crusade, Elijah Broom's Crusade, so that he may have some kind of full life, so that he may fulfill his destiny, so that I may serve some good purpose in this world and walk across the street.

We were encamped on the shores of a lake that was so large we could not see the other side, even standing on the hill or climbing the oak trees that surrounded that pristine environment. It was, at last, a good place for the children. They caught many fish, and a local German farmer brought milk and cheese and asked for no payment.

Perhaps Elijah's God had delivered us here after all.

So we filled our bellies. The times looked better and Elijah had decided to start his Crusade with new ideas. He instructed me to begin larger bookings and to venture out to the town in the morning and send out wires to the far towns soliciting meetings. He wanted me to travel ahead of our group in order to make solid arrangements and post advertisements. Laz was to take over driving the car; he had just turned fifteen.

I yelled Hallelujah! The mayor of the town had agreed to our high meeting (as Elijah now wants to call the preaching) on the outskirts of the town. He was charging no fees and told me that the town folk were in need of special redemption. He had never heard of Elijah but welcomed his coming; after all, who would reject a man of God? We were on the mark for the next Saturday night.

Elijah Rising

Elijah's voice, his movements, his words, had mutated. That was what he was doing alone in his tent for hours on end–mutating, transmogrification. He had refused food for days. I often watched his little silhouette bouncing around in his tent at night; he was made large by the kerosene light.

He delivered his best sermon ever. I should have had more confidence in him. *The Word of the Lord is writ large,* he began, his right hand held up as though blessing the crowd, his left hand held up the Bible. *Behold the Golden Text*, his voice roared. *How many here can say they be a copy of Christ's life?* The crowd (there must have been over one hundred) stood silent. He waited for just the right moment. *You must welcome your wounds, not run from them! Did Jesus run from the cross?*

NO, NO, yelled the crowd.

Do you want to be born again and forever settled in the house of the Lord?

Yes, Lord, yes, Lord.

Who in this world dares to improve God's work? Do you?

No, Lord.

The sun is old, old and made by the hands of God.

Amen!

What man sayest we need a new one?

Not me, Lord.

This is the final say. This is God's word true and pure!

Then he thrust the Bible not up but out toward the crowd. They gasped, three women in the front row fainted, and a man shouted: *We know the Lord is in you.*

I have been given a true test of your belief. Elijah pulled a white cloth from his breast pocket, unfolded it, and spread it open for the crowd to see. A blood red image stared out from bone white, a crown of thorns, tears on the cheeks. Elijah had presented the crowd with a veronica.

The pictures (Elijah holding up the cloth) and direct quotes from Elijah's meeting showed up in the Dallas papers, then were picked up on the wires. Who could have known that a reporter was at our meeting? John Sparkle had been assigned by the *Times* to do a series of articles on the old time religion. He had been following Bryan, but diverted when he had heard about Elijah.

Sparkle visited Elijah one morning and asked for an interview. Elijah told him he had to see me. I do not think this man would present Elijah well; it would all be for sensation. I told him that Mr. Broom did not give interviews. He assured me that he would follow our sawdust trail whatever I said or did. He was determined to get a story and a good one.

He was like a giant vulture, that Sparkle. He wore a black hat constantly, even in the heat of the tent, the brim pulled over his eyes so that it was impossible to fathom his thoughts. While Elijah preached and the crowd moaned and fainted when he pulled out the cloth, Sparkle did not wince; he cracked a smile, and did nothing but write in the damnable book of his. I was afraid he would break us. More afraid that he would be better than me.

It was October and we left Texas and headed well into New Mexico. We were set for a powerful meeting in Albuquerque by the end of the month. Sparkle had made Elijah's Crusade an event. Every town had welcomed us and there had been standing room only out and into the surrounding circle around the tent. The people came to hear and almost did not care whether they saw Elijah jumping, yelling, or preaching with irreverence, which he rarely did anymore. His voice was simply the voice of God bolting from the clouds.

What the was the connection between faith and curiosity?

I must admit that Sparkle did not demean our Crusade. He told it true, without pretensions or embellishments, quite straight to America. He was selling Elijah to the people. He gave me a clip of his last article. It was from a Hollywood, California paper. Sparkle said the Crusade should be heard there. *Sodom and Gomorrah needs Elijah.*

So Elijah was going to be in the newsreels and it was none of my doing. A picture crew would attend the Albuquerque Crusade. I supposed that thousands and thousands of people would see the Little Black Prophet, as he had been called of late. Elijah asked me to go into town and buy him a new outfit for our biggest event. I stayed with a black suit and white shirt, a purple tie, and shiny shoes so that the people could see that his movements set him above the floor, as though he were skipping on air. Not to be outdone by Sparkle and his pals, I worked on putting out pamphlets about Elijah, in addition to a volume of his sermons. Sparkle said he knew a publisher in San Francisco who might print and distribute the items for me. I needed to talk with Elijah a little more about his life.

Elijah Rising

To think, all the time I'd been with him, I'd known almost nothing about his past before we'd met in New York. I had trusted and loved him that much.

Plainfield was on the border of Texas and New Mexico. Not fifty feet from the edge of town was a wooden sign marking the border. It was topped with the skull of a longhorn cow.

There was very little to pick from in the small general store, but I was able to get Elijah's outfit. The storekeeper said it would fit any fifteen-year old boy right fine. I could find no purple tie, so settled for a black ribbon tie worn by many of the locals. The town was bustling, wagons passed down the dirt road running through town, dust clouds whirled in the air. I walked along the wooden planks, built, I assume, for when the rains came and mud inhibited safe and clean walking. I looked into several store windows until I got to the end of the walk, where I breathed in a familiar smell. It was like seeing an old friend that you thought had died. Chocolate. Glorious, wonderful, magical chocolate. Providential, indeed, for God had led me to a candy store where an old lady, white hair falling into her face, bent over a large silver pot and stirred. She was making chocolate fudge. I bought two large bags of the batch she made the day before, stuffed a large piece in my mouth and reveled in the melting sensation as I strolled across the street.

Along with the chocolate and Elijah's new clothes, I brought back an announcement of another meeting that was going to take place outside town the following night. Do as many people know about our Crusade as the crusade of one Hiram Wesley Evans?

Article for the Dial:

Hiram Wesley Evans is a dentist, a man schooled and licensed in what most of us in America consider an honorable and, in this part of the country, a lucrative profession. But Hiram is more than a puller of rotten teeth, he is a purveyor of rotten souls. The duly elected Imperial Wizard and Emperor of the Klan. He stands and yells at the people not far from where Mr. Bryan and Mr. Elijah Broom speak. Three men, whose purposes in captivating the souls of these desperate people are different, but whose methods are almost indistinguishable. Evans promises to save America from "furrin" control, from the alien invasion, from all that is not what he calls the "old stock." Bryan promises to save America from herself, plain and simple. Mr. Broom promises to save each soul from sin and for a restful place in heaven.

Mr. Evans must have read Lathrop Stoddard's The Rising Tide of Color, memorized passages and now hurls those words like hate on the wings of a black crow. He speaks of the migrating lower forms of life that now inhabit our shores, of the Mexican refuse that takes away the jobs of the people in this desolate land, and thus blames the "unwashed" for poverty. He exploits our fear, the one human emotion that can bring a soul to ruin and a nation to despair, for it is all nothing but hate, hate and more hate heaped upon the words that are encased in a black book. What then is the connection between America and hate?

So these Southerners have become fearful of the drunken alien, the Negro, the Jew, the man who speaks in a foreign tongue or even with an accent. It is difficult to look at the faces of the men, women and children as Evans shoots his vile words down upon them. Our politicians have given the task of community over to this man, have neglected their needs, nay, have contributed to their misery. It is a sadder-than-sad commentary on our times; for these people live in what is now a wasteland, but they, in their own way, at least see a purpose in it all. . . they see in the words of Bryan, Broom and Evans worlds larger than their own hearts.

He changed clothes right in front of me, without a sense of impropriety. His body was truly like a young boy, not slim, but unformed. His chest was hairless and wasted, his black skin looked like it had been painted on his ribs; he was no different in form than that long ago day when I saw him running toward me, the sounds of New York dashing at his side. I thought that he must have the biggest soul in the littlest body. He was beautiful and it was all I could do not to run my hands down his bony legs. He had a member that was folded away into his stomach. Surely, he was a prophet.

Then he was gone, the suit I purchased for him fit well and made him look distinguished. Elijah was going to be a crowd pleaser.

I had come to him because I was summoned, because he wanted me to write more about *The Crusade for All Time*, as he called it. *I need to know more about you, to sell you to the crowd*, I told him. *I shall tell you of my life before Jesus*, he said, *at sunup tomorrow. When the world of the Lord is coming into the first day of first light. It'll be a very good story.*

The force of love shows brightest in the morning. Elijah was right about that. I woke up before that luminous streak of light had severed the blue sky. My sleep had been anxious, going in and out of dreams that made little sense, but that had terrified me with rumbling sounds and a kaleidoscope of colors. I was, at long last, to hear the story of Elijah's life.

He knelt under the willow tree, his head bowed toward the rising sun, his hands covering his forehead. I could not hear his prayer for the cascading waters of the creek. But I watched him, my heart leaping in my breast as he swayed from side to side and then back and forth. The rhythm could have thrown me into a dreamless sleep. *Come and pray with me, Michael man*, he whispered. And I did. A prayer I set down here and will forever hold in my mind.

> *Lord, without you there is nothing, an empty universe, no clouds in the sky, a blackness blacker than the eyes of Satan. From you we draw strength to endure our trials, to make from the clay of our bodies straight walking creatures who love this land whether it be dry like Egypt or wet like the great flood. Thank you for giving me a friend in Michael. He is my keeper, your instrument, that carries out your word.*

And finally, The Story of Elijah's Life Before Jesus Came Into Him:

Lyn LeJeune

You know, Michael man. I never did 'member anything until Jesus came to me. It . . . well, it kinda like I weren't ready to carry the pain of it. Then one morning, I wake up, and I know I was ready and happy for it, too. You ever feel that? You want to know what made it come about?

After Mama died, I ran up and down those Satan-plagued streets 'til I cain't run no more.

Then I hear a big booming voice, somebody there is telling about Jesus be the Lord and he be the Lord. It was in Harlem, on a street corner. Cain't 'member what one. I ask a little girl who say he God. God done come to Harlem. I didn't believe it then, I don't believe it now, but what came over me was that if dis man can say that God be here in the hell pit, and people listen, there must be something to it. I don't know, but I was so hungry my head was spinning. Then a big hand took my shoulder and led me to a car and dis pretty white lady opened a basket and it be full of food. Man, Michae, man, it be the first time I ever bit down on a ham sandwich like dat one. Well, it was Bell and his friend. Ethel. More dan friend, fo sure. But he took me with him and I learned and listened. Yeah, I know, God appoints fools to spread the Word sometimes.

But after a while, every night I start to 'member when I was a baby, and faces, and Mama's voice, and a brown house. It all came rollin' down to me, more and more memories. I became a free man, Michael. Freedom is a memory. What is life without memories of what we are? They be good or bad. Don' matter.

Mama's hands touching me came first. I think I went way back even to when I was born. They say a man cain't 'member that. But I do. She lift me up high, and there the blood ran down her arms and the big vein thing was still running with blood. Then she put me on her breast and I

137

lived. The room was always hot and the big fireplace scared me. One time she wopped me when I went to put my hand too close. And my bothers and sisters. I wonder if Sister is alive. But they all ate at the table . . . all of us together every meal. . . with Mama. Ben, Juda, Buddy, Smith, Livia, Touch, Blue, and Sister and me. Nine babies my Mama brought to the world. Nine that lived. I think we had mor'n one daddy. I cain't tell you which went with which. But mine I know was mean as the devil. The drink done it to him. And the white man and the work in the fields. Sometimes I think I cain't blame his angry ways. I 'member him, too. Big man, with a big head and green eyes. He was a red one of us. Red bone. I was most afraid of his hands 'cause he hit so hard. Anyway, he was gone one day and Mama ain't say a word one way or another and we all sure was happy then. Juda was a good worker and he had a good boss man that gave him lots of food to bring home. I think I loved Judd mor'n anybody 'cept Mama. He sang to me. Made up songs about birds and flowers and all the natural things around us.

Juda. I love to say his name even today. Juda, Juda, Juda. Went to the army when the war came and never came back. Ben, too. Broke Mama's heart. Buddy run off. We don' know where to. Smith and Livia died when that influenza came. Touch and Blue got married and went off to Louisiana. Sister took off to the north saying she be sending us money soon. So, it be me and Mama left. She talked all the time about the north and how we could have a good life there. Kept reading me papers about good jobs for the Negro. She could read and tried teaching best she could. Said I could be a doctor and even a store owner in the north. But I had to read and get educated.

Well, one mornin' she made me get dressed in my best and she put on that pretty yellow hat with daises. She had two suitcases and bags of food ready. Said les' go little one, we

138

off to the big city. New York. Gonna find a job and put you in school. Sister had been sending a little money now and then and Mama been saving.

So we got on the train and I cried 'til my heart done broke in two. Had to leave my Pete. My dog Pete. Ain't been telling you all the things went on during the years, but I wrote it all down best I can write. I think maybe you can figure what I be trying to say. Maybe one day you can fix it.

Tell about me to the world.

We stayed on the train fo days and then had to get on and off maybe three times. Full of soldiers and other people going to camps fo the war. Me and Mama had to ride in the cow cars. Mama sure was spittin' mad 'cause she paid full price for the Negro good car. But didn't do any good how much she complained. We ran out of food that Mama had packed after three days.

Boiled up eggs and turnips and brown bread and some cheese. I was sho hungry. A porter, Sam, brought us food. I think maybe he stole the leftovers from the fancy cars. I think you know the rest. No job, no school and we never did find Sister. You know, I think Mama thought she'd get off the train and the streets would be paved with gold and there would be standing sweet Sisterl in a blue dress. Po Mama, with them bad dreams that came to her.

I had never told Elijah that his mother never made it back to Alabama. So I told him. He put his hand on my shoulder, gently shook me, then smiled. *I know that. Nobody take the body of a dead Negro woman on a train with the war dead needing the space.*

He had told me a good story, and I knew he had made much of it up just for effect.

Elijah Rising

Again my concern for Liza reared its head. She was a beauty and I'd seen the way men looked at her, white or Negro. She had to leave, be safe, hide. No, grow, but not in this part of the country. Liza had been cared for by Mama Jones ever since her mother disappeared when she was just a baby. I had discussed my plan with Mama, and she agreed. Elijah seemed not to care. My plan: Send Liza to Mother.

Dear Mother: I am writing to ask you a great favor.

There is a young girl who has traveled with us. She is an orphan and is named Liza. I fear dreadfully night and day for her life, her body, her soul. She is growing into a beautiful young woman and I fear if she stays with us she will become a rag to be wrung out by the thugs that ride through the countryside. Or she will be reduced to young motherhood and death or starvation. Either way, Mother, I know she will perish.

I am sending her to you. Please accept this act of charity. Use my trust money and your influence to get her into one of those Negro schools for girls, like the one in Daytona I heard about. Look up a Doctor Mary Bethune. Isn't this your namesake? You know influential people in New York and Florida. Work a miracle, Mother. Please, please do not let her become a servant. Give her a chance in this world, in a place that she may thrive. Do this Mother. Think of Miss Susan B. Anthony. Surely she did not draw a color line. Suffrage is for every woman, is it not? I know that when you look into Liza's eyes, see her smooth skin, her grace, her carriage, you, too, will be convinced of her destiny. She can read well even now, for I have assisted her, and she clutches my old volume of Emerson's poems to her day and night. I finally presented it to her as a gift. I inscribed it for her, November 1, 1923, directly under yours, To my son, Christmas, 1913.

But she needs to know her own people's poetry, does she not Mother?

I will put her on the train in Albuquerque (we will be there soon for the Great Revival that will be on the newsreel) bound for New York and will wire you the itinerary and her passage. I will talk to the Pullman that work on the train and they will keep an eye on her all along the lines, I'm sure of that. They are a kind lot. Meet her at the station. I have told her how wonderful you are. (Despite our sorrowful past). I know that I am doing this without your consent. But I trust you will not let me down. Nor Liza. Nor common decency. Your son.

Always, Michael.

That was the one great thing I had done in all of my life.

Thanks to Sparkle (and I never thought I'd like the fellow) we have arrived in Albuquerque safe and sound. We boarded the train, our slim belongings packed and stored along in the back cars, as was most of our crew. Only Sparkle and I were allowed rides on the front cars, and I decided it best I stay with Elijah and our gang. *Suit yourself* was all Sparkle said as he headed up to the dining car, his big cigar spewing sweet smoke in my face.

I was worse off for the worry about the big revival we were putting on in December. Elijah didn't seem to worry a bit about the arrangements or our reception. He was high in his own mind and soul and did nothing but read from his Bible, mumbling words that were foreign to me, another language only he and his Lord knew.

Albuquerque. I was amazed, surprised, pleased. I had anticipated moving soundly and forlornly into a desert where life was hard and we would see a repeat of the poverty of the farmlands, the hardness of its people. But here the railroad had gathered parts of this world into a frenetic and garish oasis. It was a new town, and the area around the station was called New Town. A plaza where all kinds of people and dress milled together. White and red and black. When we emerged from the train, Elijah held his Bible to his breast, touched my shoulder with his forehead and asked me *now Michael man, do you believe Jesus is with us?* So, I thought, Albuquerque New Mexico is Eden. And to think, we got to Eden rumbling through the Sandia Mountains and the dry desert, dab next to the Rio Grande, the river of life, riding on the iron horse financed by the men in gray suits and high hats.

What then is the connection between God and money?

We had a world of preparation, so I decided that I could learn a thing or two from Sparkle. He seemed to have more ins with the influential people in the city. So I went along with him to his haunts and dins of drink. So much for the prohibition in the wild west. I had been able to turn away from my old friend Mr. Rye during my years with Elijah. But that day I drank until I was dizzy; the old feeling had come back and I loved it again. The poverty that stalked the hinterlands and the hardness of the people in the small towns beyond these mountains did not reside in the streets of Albuquerque; it was a happy town. Swelled by foreigners, many who had come to take cures in the sanatoriums that had sprung up in the area. Could the influenza be cured here? Can only the rich afford to be cured?

Mama Jones had packed Liza's few possessions. It was time for Liza to leave us. I had received a wire from Mother letting me know that she had found a place for Liza in the Bethune Florida School. Liza would be funded by the New York Women's Guild for Negro Girls. And by Mother.

I took Liza around the Plaza to purchase new clothes. I ignored the stares and brought her into the stores along 7 and 8 Street. She held my hand, her wide eyes taking in every movement, every person that passed us by. She was not afraid and told me so. She looked forward to her journey and told me that she already loved Mother for what she had done for her. Then she asked why I did not love my mother and I could not answer, because I knew exactly why and it wasn't something a man tells a little girl.

Liza trembled with excitement when I raised her by the waist and set her on the edge of the train steps. My fingers nearly touched, that is how small she still was. I felt the little nibs of her spine. She wore a pink dress with a green sash edged with white lace. And shoes, black leather with buttons up to the middle of her calf. A hat with red cherries and green sprigs. Mama Jones had scrubbed her until she yelled, and we laughed at the wafting odor of lye soap. I think Mama wanted to lighten Liza up just a little. But she was a beauty that could never be changed.

Elijah hugged Liza as they said good-bye last night, and he had placed his hand on her head and silently told her to go with God. He smiled and rubbed her cheeks as though he knew that her fate would be good. Good. A good fate is all we ask from in this world, I think. *Are you afraid?* he asked her. *No*, she said. *This is my adventure, Preacher Broom. You had yours, now I have mine.*

I never saw Liza again. Ten years later she went to Germany to sing gospel in a new church headed by the Reverend Jedidiah Jackson. It was 1933 and she was murdered the night the glass was shattered and the knives came out in Germany.

The Great Crusade was scheduled for December 23 . . . by Sparkle. Our itinerary had been taken out of my hands. I complained to Elijah. Patience, he told me, with that misty smile that had taken over his face like a ghost. Like Hamlet to the graves.

Sparkle swept Elijah across the sky like Moses gone mad in the desert. Each day, each month, the yellow eyes of his grew deeper, brighter, almost green. His head was bent toward the rising sun, his Bible clutched against his chest. In other men, I would think that the head and heart were at war for a soul, but not in Elijah. There was both purity and sin in him. I could see his book pulse with his heart. Five angelic ducks descended into the lake, swooping over this godly man. Had he summoned them himself or had God sent them to keep him company? Better animals for the field than man. Elijah's face appeared on every street corner; *Come to the Great Crusade and hear the famous preacher Elijah Broom. Come early and get a front row seat if you want to be saved. It's only a thin dime extra.*

Elijah's voice had grown deeper than ever. A mammoth sound from a tiny sparrow body. He no longer prayed to God, but invoked the spirit of the wind. His countenance had become ethereal, his dark skin

143

now shadow-gray, the little silhouette I had first seen on the streets of New York with a power beyond words. Sometimes, when I looked at him in that state of his damaged innocence, I felt a deep pain, agonizing, as though I were being called to another world for my role in selling Elijah. I had lost myself in Elijah's life and had lost my own. Gone were the days when I spoke ill of the moneychangers in the temple; I had become one myself. I had railed against the shortcomings of the world, had envied others, and then one morning I woke only to realize to my great horror that I had let grow in my own heart the same evils I had scorned.

The rehearsal lasted more than an hour, with Sparkle standing behind the tent pretending he was one of the flock. That damned hat and the infernal toothpick bobbing in his mouth sent me into an inner rage. I was jealous. I had been given the job of writing the revival prayers for distribution; really I merely copied Elijah's words. It seemed as though that was all I was good for. Again my anger got the best of me. Why was Elijah never angry? He had suffered more than anyone I knew.

Where had time gone? It was like I'd drawn a line in the sand, saying this is my lifeline, and it is that which tells me where yesterday ends and tomorrow begins. Christmas was upon us already. Albuquerque was decorated and the new stores peddled their wares with bright lights and intriguing goodies. I decided to shop and buy a few presents. I realized as I stood at the candy trays that I had not felt the pain of my stomach in almost a year, not even when we had only collards and bone soup to eat. Surprising, since the food that I now ate was dripping with fat; it was often hard to even find meat on the bone. I had learned to eat the fat and suck the bone. For Elijah I got Claude McKay's *Harlem Shadows*; for Mama Jones, Billy Sunday's *Love Stories of the Bible*, and for myself, O'Neill's *Emperor Jones*.

Temperate weather served to ensure a large turnout for the Great Christmas Crusade. The wind had died down to a gentle breeze, the moon was bright, and fireflies danced around the tent in a cascade of shimmering rivers. There must have been over a thousand people in attendance. We had strung out colored lights from the tent entrance and down a walkway some twenty feet. *Welcome to the Lord's Great Crusade*, read our large banner. Gaiety and fun was the mood until Elijah came on the platform. The laughter and mumbling stopped abruptly, faces turned upward to receive the word, a story to be told over and over in the quiet of sleepless nights or to banish boredom in barber shops. Elijah was in top form. Sparkle was ready with pen and paper. The newsreel men stood in front of the tent. I took in a breath and prayed before he opened his mouth, threw out his hands, that all would be well. But I could not shake the fear that possessed me among a crowd that did not have much to lose if they turned against Elijah.

Elijah delivered what he had decided to call the *Blood On the Water Sermon*: *Who is ready to take Jesus into his soul? Say it, say it now, say, Jesus come into my soul. Walk across the River Styx, follow the Lord, put your faith deep down in Jesus, a head full of thorns, I cry and the Lord is with us. Accept the Lord now, now, now.* He threw the words at the crowd like bolts of lightening, yelling and jumping, sweat pouring from his face, the people fainting and crying and then Elijah spoke in words that were not words, syllables that made no sense. He had come to speak in tongues, foreign, joyful and dangerous. How would this go over? What would Sparkle write? Why had Elijah not told me his plan? Was this human intention or divine intervention?

Christmas day was joyful. We all agreed that the Christmas sermon inspired the people. Elijah believed that Jesus had entered many souls. Sparkle said that Elijah was ready for Hollywood and Elijah said that the newsreel would reach many souls.

Despite all we had endured on the road, the losses and the hunger and nature. . . the cold and the heat . . . We all rejoiced in our future. Elijah decided that it was time to lay out a new plan for the New Crusade in Hollywood. He was moving too far afield and would not listen to me that he would become nothing more than entertainment. *My destiny is preordained, God leads me*, said Elijah. And I replied: *Sparkle is Faust.*

WHEN ELIJAH COMES

I got brains and I uses 'em quick. Dat ain't luck.
—The Emperor Jones

Elijah Rising

When I was a boy, well it doesn't really matter where except down south, I met an old man. He always sat at the right of a dirt road, rain or sunshine, at the exact time the bus passed bringing the white kids to school. I wasn't interested in that movement of life; it just wasn't my provenance. But Mama had shoed me out of the house, told to get on outa der so she could clean. We lived in a two-room shack that was cold in winter, hot in summer; the dang thing couldn't seem to make up its mind what it wanted to be. Daddy plugged the holes in the rotten wood as though that act would force a decision, or perhaps he knew way back then that the barbarians were coming. He shouldn't have bothered; first, he disappeared after giving me the worst shellacking I'd ever had, and second they came anyway, the barbarians, and there was nothing we could do to stop them.

It was the hour or so after the beating and I could finally slip from my Mamma's bed, crawl out of the house, and stand on my wobbly legs. I took off down the road, fell, got up, and there he was. Old man watching the white kids again. I sat next to him only because I couldn't walk too good. I looked down the road and he said: *Ain't come yet.* He handed me his bottle of corn liquor and I took a long drink and boy did that feel good. Slowed the pain for a while.

Ole man, I said, *why you be hera lookin' at dem white kids evera day? Ain't you business.*

He coughed and spit out a glob right on my dirty foot. I picked up some dirt and cleaned it off. *I want to see where dey goin'*, he said.

How in hell cain ya see dat if you sit in one place.

I knows, I knows dey goin' to Elysian Fields.

What be dat? I asked him. I stood up ready to take off to find my friends when the old man grabbed my hand and pulled me down.

Sit hera chil' and I tells ya a story.

Nothing else to do, I thought, so I stayed. And this is the short version of the story he told me:

There was once a town with many white children all born at the same time. They were fat and pink-faced with pudgy arms and legs. They all had eyes that were sure to turn blue, or a least a misty green. The mothers wanted to be modern, to raise their children like they thought the rich did over in a place called The East. The mothers all got together and decided that their past use of black mamas to feed their babies was wrong. After all, didn't a doctor write something about diseases and blood passing from one race to another? Surely there's a little blood in breast milk, especially when a baby gets teeth and bites away. Hard to see blood on a black breast. But the idea of feeding their babies themselves, well, that was a bit disgusting. So they made a decision to feed their babies something called powdered milk.

Well, said the old man, *dat be like saying howdy to dissolution.*

Anyway, the babies were fed from bottles and it was so easy to be a mama. They could just put the bottle on a pillow next to the babies and do something else, get their housework done, for example. The children grew, but their legs were spindly, there cheeks no longer rosy. And the worst thing happened: Not one of the children spoke one word.

Now how can you have a world without words?

I told the old man, *dat silly. 'Magine a whole lots chiln' cain't talk.*

He looked at me and shook his head. *You cain't talk either. Listen to yoself, listen to me. Dem white kids on da bus talk a language eryone can undastand.*

I talk good, I huffed.

No you ain't.

He continued his story. He said that the mothers forgot one thing when they decided to feed their children from bottles. God existed before language; God gives man language to come together, to be one in Christ. Without words and words every day and for every situation, we would be like beasts.

Okay, I'll say it, like the barbarians.

Well, just about that time the bus came trundling down the road, spreading gravel and dust all over the place and when it passed me and the old man it hit a puddle and near about drowned us in mud. But I got the chance to see the faces of the children as the bus slowed with the hole it had hit. They all seemed to have white or red hair, they faces looked like spooks, their eyes blue and green and soft, without comprehension of what they were even looking at.

See der, said the old man, *deys empty. Now doin't let dat happen to ya. Speak boy, learn da language. So far ya doin' havta stay a little nigger boy and die in da cold.*

Then he straightened his back, stood up, and handed me the empty bottle. *Get rid of this,* he snorted. *My advice should carry you a long way. You will get along in the world, not be broken every time you turn around*

Elijah Rising

if you do two things: Pretend to be what you are not and while you're doing that always be who you are. And then he reached into his ratty coat and handed me a book.

I thought the man must have been really drunk, but his words kept coming back to me. That night I asked Mama what the man meant. She was mad as an old mule when I told her I'd been talking to him. I thought she was going to slap me and, Lord, I'd had enough from Daddy. But she pulled her hand away and wiped it on her dress. *Da black man gots da pretend ta da whites to be lowdown. But ya neva be lowdown. A man becomes wat a man does.*

I didn't show Mama the book, especially after she told me Daddy done gone and brother and sister were going to have to find some kind of work. Every night I'd sneak outside near the chicken pen and read by candle light. That was when I took to heart the advice of the old man and was determined to get through life no matter where I went. I was going to take every opportunity to act who I wasn't, but be who I was. So help me Lord.

The book was *The Souls of Black Folk* by Mr. W.E.B. DuBois. I sat with that book all night and then sometimes I hid behind the mulberry tree and read it again and again. I'd found a pencil in Mama's room and so I'd leave a little check at each word I had a hard time pronouncing. One day I made it part way through the book and all was confusion. Hell, we didn't even have a mirror so I could look at myself as others saw me, so I could learn to play the part yet become more. And there it was, the section called "When John Comes." You must read the entire thing to understand why I was shocked and why it changed my life. It was the easiest reading so far. So I marked the page and read through that story twenty times if not fifty. And that was when I learned an important lesson, one I came up with all on my own: *When I preach, I preach about myself.* I know you're saying who reads DuBois anymore. So what, it was my defining moment. I leave you with a few passages (remember that I remember to the letter everything I read) and you may understand me more fully. Imagine a little black boy, no shoes and it's cold out, a candle flutters in the night, he has read this passage twelve times already and finally he understands:

> *He looked now for the first time sharply about him, and wondered he had seen so little before. He grew slowly to*

150

feel almost for the first time the Veil that lay between him and the white world; he first noticed now the oppression that had not seemed oppression before, differences that erstwhile seemed natural, restraints and slights that in his boyhood days had gone unnoticed or been greeted with a laugh. He felt angry now when men did not call him "Mister," he clenched his hands at the "Jim Crow" cars, and chafed at the color-line that hemmed in him and his. A tinge of sarcasm crept into his speech, and a vague bitterness into his life; and he sat long hours wondering and planning a way around these crooked things. Daily he found himself shrinking from the choked and narrow life of his native town.

Surely I don't need to explain to you what that did to me, how I looked at my world with different Senses; the colors were no more black and white; I was a shade walking across the world and accepting it for all its misery. I understood how to rebel without anyone knowing at first. I understood my hard road coming, that I would suffer as well as my family. I did not see what I did not see then. Do you think I would have changed course had I known what would happen to brother and sister and Mama? I tell you now, no, I had figured out my destiny. I would speak the words beyond the Veil, not only to the black man, but to whites who had given over to despair because of their meanness. I was not going to let myself be like them.

Little had they understood of what he said, for he spoke an unknown tongue, save the last word about baptism; that they knew, and they sat very still while the clock ticked. Then at last a low suppressed snarl came from the Amen corner, and an old bent man arose, walked over the seats, and climbed straight up into the pulpit. He was wrinkled and black, with scant gray and tufted hair; his voice and hands shook as with palsy; but on his face lay the intense rapt look of the religious fanatic. He seized the Bible with his rough, huge hands; twice he raised it inarticulate, and then fairly burst into words, with rude and awful eloquence. He quivered, swayed, and bent; then rose aloft in perfect majesty, till the people moaned and wept, wailed and shouted, and a wild shrieking arose from the corners where all the pent-up feeling of the hour gathered itself and rushed into the air. John never knew clearly what the old man said; he only felt himself held up to scorn and scathing denunciation for trampling on the true Religion, and he realized with amazement that all unknowingly he had put rough, rude hands on something this little world held sacred.

Do you see how this changed me, how I wanted to be like the old man, but not like him? How I wanted to shake John and say, don't you see how you have to be? False prophets never make it through the Veil of tears, because they let themselves be known. I was bent on giving the white world what it expected, and then along the way I would make it to the Promised Land. I would end up in Hollywood, and become the real Al Jolson.

DuBois ends his story about John with these words: *And the world whistled in his ears.* Was he not prescient? I am writing at the time after Emmett Till whistled at a white woman, let the world know who he was straight on, and for that he paid with his life. I would not hear about Emmett for years, but I always heard the world whistling in my ears.

And so when Michael came into my life he served a purpose, the Beriah Green to the soon to be Elijah Broom. I knew from the moment I met him that Michael man knew so little of himself and of men in general. So I acted the part, scaled the buildings and icy streets until I had convinced him that I needed him. And thus began his search. Yes, I left New York and traveled south and then west, because I knew the territory, understood that the black people there were hungry for a prophet; it was what they were raised on after the ships landed on the southern shores and the masters and priests persuaded them of their fate. I would tell them, as DuBois wrote, that there would soon be a reckoning, a *final NO.*

So I let Sparkle use me and in that act I hurt a true friend. I knew that I would have to abandon him; he had performed good works for me, was the perfect left hand. But now, with Sparkle, I had found my right hand man. For those of you who are clucking your tongue and calling me soulless or wicked, perhaps even usurious, remember the times in which I lived; do you seriously think that I could have survived by following the rules of the white man?

How did I let Michael down? How did I get him to leave and go on his own way? It was so easy. I simply ignored him, perhaps once and a while giving him a chore. I let him use me for his articles, it all went into creating Elijah Broom. With Michael and Sparkle together, well, I was, as they say, a shoe in.

I have to say that along our journey, I paid little attention to what was happening with our gang. One day I woke up and Liza was gone. The death of Smith did throw me off course, but his death merely proved my point and steeled me even more to my task.

I loved the meetings, I loved preaching to the people, I loved the looks on their faces when I jumped up, and don't think I didn't know what some of them white folks were thinking. I had vowed to something after I'd read DuBois. I knew the souls of black folk; I was one of them. My aim was to know the souls of white folk. That was the first thing a black man had to do in those times to stay alive.

Michael did me great service by taking me to see Williams Jennings Bryan and Hiram Wesley Evans. Who ever thought I'd learn from the grand Wizard of the Klan. But often in war, you just have to use the same weapons as the enemy and, along the way, make them better. My tools came from myself and the tools of the modern age. Yes, the moving pictures, the automobile, which got me to where I was going faster than I could imagine, and the American fear of the alien, which was no more than a fear of themselves. Of course, I count me as one, an American, and I was intent on making my mark. Perhaps in the end I was that boy, Alexander Crummell, who moved on without despair when *the godly farmers hitched ninety yoke of oxen to the abolition schoolhouse and dragged it into the middle of the swamp. The black boy trudged away.*

It all led up to the Great Christmas Crusade of 1923. I had succeeded. I'd pushed myself into the American dream and the white women swooned and the blacks believed in me and the white men held their guns to their sides and carried no hanging rope.

1924 and I was off to Hollywood with Sparkle.

INTO GOD'S PROVIDENTIAL CARE

I fear the plutocracy of wealth; I respect the aristocracy of learning; but I thank God for the democracy of the heart.
—William Jennings Bryan

Elijah Rising

This was Elijah's Plan and How He Delivered the Word:

He stood before us as the sun passed away into oblivion. His voice a vibration like the cello at New York Symphony. I remembered my Bach too well as he spoke, so that I could feel the agony of the future. Premonition not predestination. Black Bach. He raised up on his toes, snapped up then down, his hands thrust deeply into his pockets. I was afraid to look at his face. But what else was I to do, what choice had I confronted by the force of his love? *We will head directly west toward California, make preaching, make God's way to the people, on into the valley's and mountains and forests where trees are frozen into red rock. I have seen this in my God dreams. Then we will go where the wayfarers from the south have made their own. Each time we meet people in spiritual emptiness we will stop and fill them up. Yes, we will stop often on God's road. At last we will face the great Pacific Ocean. I see fear in your eyes. Be with me and there is nothing to fear. I have studied the maps and God's finger has shown me the way. He has moved my hand with His. His on top of mine, blood and skin and bone as one. He has told me that we will reach the Ocean on the day of his birth. YES! We shall spend Christmas of 1924 on the shores of this Great Land. A new Land. We will have crossed the desert. There God will give me the word, the final word, where I will truly cast my blood upon the waters. Ready for the great pictures that will deliver the message to the people.*

He was no longer my Elijah, my little Washington. He put his hand on my shoulder and said: *Michael man, God has told me your duty. You are to write my sermons and teach me the new ways of men like Mr. Charlie Chaplin. I shall reach the people, God's word shall reach the people, by the moving pictures and the radio. A thousand plus one more thousand and more will hear me each night from their kitchen tables and living room chairs. And when they see me high on the big picture, they will finally know that I come as the second Moses. Michael man, you will write my story for the world . . . through me from God. On waves will God's voice flow through the air. No more war, no more hate, no color to hold a man or woman back. We shall be free.*

I realized, as I lay on my cot while the early evening descended, trying to decide how and if I could do what Elijah (God) wanted, that he had probably learned something from Father Divine when he was in Harlem. To be unique was the key to it all. A disciplined life; racial

156

equality, and celibacy for men and women of God. Yes, there was some of the Divine in Elijah, and some Billy Sunday, and Jesus, and just about any holy ordained person I could think of. But Elijah was still too aloof now to appeal to the common man. He could learn that craft from Mr. Bryan. Perhaps my first chore was to teach Elijah a little American history. Speeches of our great Americans. That's what I need him to read, or read them to him. Adams, Lincoln, Roosevelt, Bryan, Wilson, James, DuBois, Randolph . . . No, he was never in repose; that would not work. He was made for the moving picture show.

But didn't I have to try? So before we left Albuquerque, I went to the city library and (forgive me) stole the books I needed. I left twenty dollars on the front desk with a note. Except James. I couldn't find William James' works. No matter.

Elijah liked Lincoln the best. Of course. Then Roosevelt. When I told him that I had sat on the president's knee when I was a boy, he said that I had been in the presence of a great man. When I told him I had thrown my food up from riding on his knee, he howled with laughter. I had seen him laugh just a few times. It was good to see that smile, the straight white teeth, the wide mouth taking in life again. But now when he laughed, the deep crevices that were telling his holy aging blasted through me like a cannon shot. Elijah was no more than twenty at the time and as old as Methuselah, as bodacious as Lazarus.

It took us almost one month to get to an encampment about fifteen miles outside of St. Johns, Arizona. We were told by two lonesome looking bums walking along the road that a great river snaked through this dry land, then beyond were thick forests. Indian Territory. Apache. Then Flagstaff, where we were to meet the feral Sparkle again. The roads were rough and lightly traveled. We had to stop every time we saw any possibility of getting gas for our autos. I have never met such an unfriendly lot of people in this country; suspicious and frightening. Every child that I saw had hollowed out eyes, big and bright, that looked at the world as though a monster were about to jump out of the sky and gobble them up. It was a sensation that struck home with me: somehow, somewhere I had seen these children before.

157

Elijah Rising

I got tired of reading to Elijah. He insisted on our nightly sessions and I swear I had read Lincoln to him so many times it made me dizzy each time I started up again. I thought he was memorizing the speeches, but now that the years had passed I realized that he wasn't even listening to me. He simply aged before my eyes, his voice became deep as though he were blowing through a trumpet.

I should not disparage the new territory. It was the most beautiful sight I had ever seen and totally biblical. I was more weary now than I'd been in years. It was like the influenza time when I had knocked softly on death's door. And the morning scenery was all that grabbed me to life. Our encampment overlooked a desert full of blue and orange rocks that soaked up the sun. Moon dust had gathered here at just this time, just for Elijah, for eons. This was where the life force waited, in the desert. The speared cacti gave us moisture and had revived the small children. We are twenty left in the Crusade. None seemed happy anymore, not since Albuquerque, and I had heard my people whisper under the tall ponderosa pines at night saying that we should have headed south to the waters of Texas. They were afraid of this endless orange land.

We did not rest but traveled on ten miles and ever closer to Flagstaff. I still didn't trust Sparkle; I thought that he had abandoned us. This desert was hot and frightening. He wasn't going to be in Flagstaff; it was all a game, a wicked, wicked trick.

Elijah finally came out of his moody silence to talk to us. He stood near the unhallowed firelight, the singing of the coyote echoed through the air. Beyond the canine calling, hoary sounds of drums pounded, an historical sound that brought us all to the edge of time, pictures of black bodies in boats reflected in Elijah's eyes. There was anger there for the first time since I had looked into those cobalt eyes. *If you leave, you leave God. Our journey is just beginning. Over them hills and through the dry earth awaits a promise*, he said. *I have spent my life banging ploughshares into words. I have denied those I have regarded better sustenance. I shall never enter the Land of Nod. I move on to the end. Come with me if you choose it.*

When I looked at the reflection of the young men jumping in the night light, I saw confusion. This new language that Elijah had taken on was strange. They blinked continuously, as though they were summoning ancient understanding. All that was left when Elijah went back to his tent

158

was a sense of loss. The gang had given Elijah many generosities, and his proffer was abandonment. One boy folded his hand and mumbled, surely praying for guidance; and not from Elijah.

So then what is the connection, Elijah, between preaching and prayer?

The next morning we came across more than fifty dead bison. Slanted, black, forbidding eyes stared out at the sky that had watched the dispersing of their seed for thousands of years. Dead and gone. Four men on horseback were pulling them into a circle by ropes. They sold us a side of meat for two dollars. Mama cooked stew for our evening meal. It was a bitter yet satisfying taste. Elijah did not eat with us; he had started to fast.

Five more days and we were near Flagstaff. I looked up the road and saw a bright light shining up into the desert sky. I heard the railroad rumbling, the yelp of a gray fox, the rustle of a running jackrabbit, the hoot of an owl. The night should have been cool, but it was hot and arid. It was only March. The stars shook in the black sky, like white holes on velvet cloth. All was blinks of life, not the cold ice of stars and planets. All, all was solitude here on earth.

When we woke up the next morning four of our young men had gone. They had vanished into the desert and I only hoped that they went straight to Flagstaff. The land could eat a man up quickly. I felt Elijah at may back, and for the first time I wanted to admonish him, yell: don't you see, Washington? Poverty robs a man of hope.

But I did not. We packed up and headed to Flagstaff. We came upon a wagon piled high with Indian artifacts. Pothunters. Two hard white men asked us if we lost four nigger boys aways back. Elijah approached the wagon, his eyes narrowed, his now white head thrust upward toward the men and asked

They be dead then, man?

Yep, deader dan a shit buckeye.

They had been found tied to an ancient barbed fence that ran for miles along a shallow creek. A local Indian (they said he was a Hopi) had taken them down and covered them with branches from a tree; green leaves soaked up our friends' blood, and the leaves and the bodies turned a deep purple. The muscles in Elijah's arms bulged when we lifted the bodies onto our wagon, and it was as though I no longer had a part in their lives, nor in their deaths, and surely not in their travels through eternity.

Elijah Rising

Elijah decided that they should be buried out in the wilderness as soon as possible. So, we turned toward the setting sun and traveled into nothingness for about an hour. A patch of cacti, their yellow blooms like gaslights, reflected the bright orange light of the coming dusk. I wondered how in God's heaven the two of us were to dig four graves before dark.

The night descended without my noticing, simply because a white moon had taken the place of the sun, its gleams bathing Elijah's face with ancient slivers of light. His face had turned golden brown, fire lit his eyes, and I felt tremors like he had become his own ancestor, who would rain fire and damnation upon earth's sinners.

Kneeling next to the graves, Elijah held my hand. I felt again the power of this man to change my life. He squeezed and chanted over and over again: *Vengeance is mine sayest the Lord*, until even the moon had vanished and the coyotes stopped their nightly crying. We left the boys in the desert, and headed back to the encampment to tell our already bleak crew that God had ordained for us more trials and tribulations.

How long did it take me to finally realize that life was pain, it was sorrow, it was time reflected backward? What kind of man had I become? Who will go with Dante and me into this hell? Word of God . . . word of civilization . . . word of Man . . . amen. I had loved Elijah to the point of a broken heart, and he was leaving me. Preaching was nothing more than a magic act.

Sparkle arrived at our encampment all in a high mood. He told us that the newsreels were a great hit. Maybe Elijah could be the religious Al Jolson. I cringed at this blasphemy and could not see why Elijah would go along; but I knew that he would. I was bone tired and bone dry and left the encampment for solitude and hopped a Harriman Coach up to the Grand Canyon. This was God's creation, surely, but desolate, a place were the fallen angels resided.

Sparkle booked us on the Atlantic and Pacific bound for California. We were to leave in two weeks.

Elijah had started to write his sermons and he asked me to correct his writing for eventual publication. Of course the language was rough, but it was also infused with a spirit that the world did not deserve. The people that Elijah had preached to so far understood his actions more than word; sin and sinners and precious blood of Christ. The wider audience would never appreciate his fire . . . demented, divine, God, born in the

160

Lord, walk with Jesus. This was a Christian nation, no doubt, but the people walked with steel and iron and guns. Nothing had changed since the Civil War and beyond.

My thoughts were scattered. A yellow dog limped into our encampment one morning seeking a piece of fat I had thrown into the underbrush. With a swish of the branches, out the poor fellow came, the gristle tightly locked in his mouth. He walked up to me and deposited it at my feet. Elijah reached out, pulled the dirty dog to him, kissed it on the snout and said: *You be Pete, sure and fine, Pete.*

Such care for a dog.

The article from the San Francisco paper lay on my cot, torn out, the serrated edges like a dog's angry teeth. *The Simian Preacher* screeched the headlines. Well, at least California had class; from monkey to simian. Sparkle had taken a photograph of Elijah at the Christmas Crusade just as he had jumped, his legs splayed and behind and between his legs was a dark, long shadow. It looked like a tail. How was I to tell Elijah about this, about his life and the series of betrayals he must face? My guilt was that I helped bring him this far. I was his Judas.

But Elijah laughed at the picture, saying that God sure worked in strange ways. At least his message would be out. *Did Jesus turn away from the moneychangers?* He asked me. No, he went into their house and showed the world what they were.

I decided to confront Sparkle. I told him that he was a disgrace to writers, that he was using Elijah for his own gain. He puffed on an infernal black cigar, smiled, and said that he was what America was all about, *it's all a big show, life, isn't it, Michael man.* Sparkle had convinced Elijah to put on a tent show the Saturday before we were to leave for California. I objected. We were not ready. The town had not been properly notified. Who would come? Newspapers, cameras, and movie moguls were coming, said Sparkle, *and who cares about the little people. Elijah is on the big train to the movies. And money.*

Shame, fiasco, evil, what other words can I describe what happened that last night? Sparkle introduced Elijah, called him a little man of God, the Chaplin of the tent preachers. He told the crowd (there must have been over a thousand people) that they should smile, clap hard, show that God is going right into them. The newsreel people were in full force.

Elijah Rising

Sparkle promised that the event would appear at the Fox Theater in San Francisco.

I was infuriated, told Elijah this was all wrong. Oh, to have had my old friend rye at that moment!

I had wanted to post guards, but none could be had for one dollar or two or ten. They were as elusive as ghostly children in white sheets. I heard the old whispers in my ear, and imagined that the corn could talk to me. I feared that I was losing Elijah and my old, crazy voices were coming back.

As I smoked outside of the tent, I heard Elijah yell *I am God's little fool* and the people yelled and laughed. And then he started his Bryan speech and crosses of gold and Lincoln and the freedom of the body and soul and Roosevelt and this great country. On and on he ranted, the tent swayed when the songs of redemption started. Oh, unholy night!

We were to leave for California in the morrow. Mama Jones and the rest of the crew would not be coming with us. Sparkle allowed Elijah to give them a substantial amount of money, enough to keep them going for at least a few months. I would miss them, especially Mama. Pete would come with us and could ride in the freight cars. We had very little possessions to take with us. I had my black carpetbag, my leather satchel with my journals and books, and I was ready.

I must have been drugged, poisoned, loaded on the train, but not the one bound for California. They sent me back home. I woke up in a sleeping car as the train pulled into the station at Lynchburg. I had slept for days, my head felt as though an anvil had fallen on me. I should have known that Sparkle wanted Elijah as his own commodity. I had twenty dollars in my pocket, my bags lay beside the narrow bed, and under the pillow was a bottle of corn whiskey. The kindness of the betrayer!

So, there I was, where I began, in a small apartment on the East Side of New York. Mother acquired the apartment for my rest. After all, she owns the building.

And what of Elijah? He was a famous product of this great and glorious country. In the newsreels, on stage, bringing religion to Babylon.

Indian summer descended early this year.

Lyn LeJeune

I visited Mother.

I went to my old haunts in the village. I saw prosperity and happiness, no more rants for the red revolution, rage against the poverty that haunted the slums. The Village and the Club were full of fun. The east had yet to merge with the other side of America.

Father died. Shot through the head by his lover, sleek Nita. It was a juicy scandal for the tabloids. Father left everything to Mother. It was part of the deal they had made years ago. I was rich, more than rich when mother died too. It would be a burden.

If I write his name I will die. There he was as he was in the beginning, a moving, flipping picture of a man, larger than my life, still blasting the word to the world that listens not to his words, but to the inflection, the tone, the blackness of his skin. Black and white is all there is in front of me now, a clown before Valentino, an imitation of Jolson. If I could, I would thrust my fist into Sparkle's heart and pull it out for the world to see. There, there is your blackest heart! But it was my chest that was empty.

Ghosts waited for me here. I heard them night and day now, in hallways, in the streets, in my bed. I could not escape. And it was the colors of life that assaulted me most heinously. Streaks of light and color and then I could taste sweet sausage and mint. I consumed the best chocolates and had boxes spread throughout my new apartment. I drank and died each night, falling again into the old days of oblivion, the days before Elijah. The dreams had started; dreams that did not stop even when the edge of day sliced through my window, leaving trails of silver blood on my bed.

I suppose I should have told the mayor of Rio that Elijah was a Negro. When Elijah jumped onto the stage the crowd muttered and turned away from him. Those who stayed, the good clean and white Christians, yelled obscenities and soon started throwing dirt and dried dung at him. I jumped on the stage. I saw myself, clad in gray wool, with white gloves and tried to drag him away. I can still feel the touch of his hot body. Elijah, I yelled and yelled, come off, they will hurt you, kill you. He pulled away from me, the strength of many men, and his preaching grew louder, as though the sound of a churning reel had been turned to high. Elijah, call forth God's angels. None came. Silence descended, a cobalt sky whirled around just Elijah and me. The few people that stayed, moved backward, away from us, stared at Elijah's little stick figure, prostrate on the wooden stage. All hope had fled, even for these few who could not laugh. All hope . . . gone.

I woke to a morning that was as cold as a mule's ass. Crimping, grinding, shit of a New York cold! I'd be damned to eternal hell here alone. Go away I tell you! I'm hungry already, and I fed you night and day and day and night. Go the fuck away from me!

Time to make my contribution to the orphans of this fine and unique city. I have arranged with my lawyers to build a new orphanage on the property Mother so kindly gave me as part of my inheritance. No child, no child, no kind of child, shall be turned away. Each will have the finest education possible, good food, and glorious, wonderful heat! What kind of man am I who can at least purchase his way into heaven?

Lost souls that walk the streets of New York, sleek bodies, cloaks covering the glaring sun, laughing specters. This morning I saw them copulating against a wall that had become green from cold and damp; or was that from their stinking bodies? The man whispered to her, see this? Do you want it? They panted, like horses in a race for their bygone lives, like Elijah after his Friday Sermons. Then the smell of mushrooms, meat on my tongue, the brine filled barrel overturned and green and yellow pickles roll over the cragged bricks. Yes, that's it ducky, lovely. Howls, cigarette smoke. I am helpless here. Exiled.

What a great show. The Macy's Christmas Day parade, with mechanical toys, bright colors, laughing faces. I shall purchase toys for my orphanage. A small boy with yellow eyes, face turned up to stare at me. It was Washington all over again. I cried to see him come back. He took my hand, or did I take his? and I led him back here for only one reason. I gave him a toy circus, still wrapped, protected, useless to me now.

THE OPENING DOOR

Elysium is as far as to
The very nearest room,
If in that room a friend await
Felicity or doom.

What fortitude the soul contains,
That it can so endure
The accent of a coming foot,
The opening of a door.
—Emily Dickinson

Elijah Rising

Will climbed the tree. He had to go so high. Then he loosened the ropes from around the purple wrists. I watched Elijah's body descend towards me. I held out my arms. The white cloth received him. He is so tiny. The weight of who he was pressed me into the earth. My knees folded and I fell to the ground. My body rested over his, lightly, as though I had become but a feather. At last, I held him in my arms . . . now and at the hour of our death. I saw it all so long ago, in the eyes of your Mama in a dank room in this city that is here and everywhere we look. They have always waited for you at the door with ropes in their hands; you who signified everything. *Dawg eats da dawg.*

Mother had sent Harold for me. I had refused to open my door for weeks now. Frankly, I think I had simply lost my grasp on life. Will let them take me for a rest cure? Sparks flew out of me. Maybe someone can help me put the fire out.

I argued and I won. The damned doctor wanted to take my journals away. To hell with him. I must leave soon. They cannot help me here.

Zelda told me that she is crazy, too. Crazy as a bat out of hell, crazy as a loon, crazy as crazy can be. Whoopee.

Again they threatened to take my journal away. You don't use them, anyway, they say. Yes, yes, I do. I write in them every day. You just can't see what I write. Why should you? You will not understand. You tear at my soul.

Doctor Fortis said I was repressed. What is repressed? Fools hide behind words. Benighted words that say nothing.

She sat near me out in the gardens now that the warmth of early spring was here. She told me she likes yellow the best, then green, then pink, then red. No, no, vermilion. Colors and sounds (she sings!!) came from her that take away my own.

I could walk out, walk along down the road on a nice morning, hitch a ride to some place else.

I absolutely despised Fortis. So did Zelda. She called him the ass in time. He's a sex fiend, she told me.

My nerves were somewhat calmed now that Doctor Fortis has adjusted my medications. Oh, how I begged that I be allowed my journals. You cannot deny me! I must write, I told him, and then I yelled until he consented. Smug bastard. Perhaps it will be good therapy, he yapped, like one of those springy dogs that nip, nip at my ankles. I spread my hands on the cool glass of the windows. The black bars were shafts piercing my hands. The world was opaque at one moment, then iridescent, and if I waited long enough, until my tongue dried and I craved wetness, it all turned brilliant and clear. Holy Father, it has been years and years and years since I have confessed my sins.

Now I am not alone. I have been given a new voice whose name is Zelda. She has helped me bring the world back into me by touching me and licking my cheeks and telling me not to be afraid. She is a laughing lady until her throat hurts, she says, and she echoes against the wall. The others yell at her to shut up, shut up, so we are taken outside. I hold it all in, I tell her. I wrap my arms around myself, squeeze hard, before my insides fly into the universe. Then I am like a meteor. I do not want to be lost again and again and again like my friend. What was his name? At a party. He died. Blown to smithereens. If it were not for her. I have known her for only three weeks.

We are compatriots in madness. We are both sent here for? What? Why are we here? I asked her yesterday. Zelda , I said, *can you at all fathom why we have been put here, after all the years we have walked through the fire?* She said because we were destined to be here, or it is just bad luck, or perhaps, one fine day, God just decided to hate us. What's the difference, we decided, between the Pope or God or Zeus or Buddha or Ra or Mohammed or Elijah, or crap, the Mountain. They all sent us straight to hell.

I see her meaning in the peonies. It is her favorite flower. She paints like the devil is in her. Like Washington and Billy Sunday when they were all fired up and panting the scriptures. Billy, you went fast and clean, but poor Washington, you got kluxed on that fiery cross. Black preacher on a fiery cross. Zelda is beautiful and full of life, whirling and hued by vermilion. I think the world is not ready for you, Zelda. The name is in the madness. Z. The last one. It's all about the fire that has left scaly scabs all over your face and neck. Mine are in my stomach, so you are not allowed to see them. You told me that you are bitched over and over by the morphine they keep giving you. I am bitched by life. Shit them.

I will tell you I love you tomorrow.

Elijah Rising

Nurse Anderson took our picture. It is here, pushed into my journal for today. See. Zelda is so tall and thin; I told her that she looked like a crazy egret, not a loon. She wears pants. Her hair falls over her right eye. And I, a little man next to her. My hair has grown long and dark over my ears. A moustache. A gray suit. We are holding hands.

IN THE FOREST OF THE NIGHT

California, Here I Come
Right back where I started from
where bowers of flowers
bloom in the spring
each morning at dawning
birdies sing at everything
a sunkissed miss said, "Don't be late!"
that's why I can hardly wait
open up that golden gate
California, Here I Come
—Al Jolson

Elijah Rising

Yes, the doctor at the sanitarium sent me a nice picture of Michael and an unnamed woman. I was always sad about what happened to Michael; he was not made for the greater stage. He was always so damned concerned about the state of my soul. I never did have the heart to tell him that I had been damned to preach. Poor Michael man, he cared how the world turned. I did not; it just never seemed to make a bit of difference. Every time I turned a corner I saw the same poverty, the same emptiness, the same cruelties. War was with us forever. All I wanted to do was save a few souls, just a few.

And along the way, yes, I lost the gift of prayer. Here in Hollywood, I do not baptize, or preach; there are no stark prayers that come to me at night. I have become an actor. I once wanted to be wise. But that is a pipe dream, as they say around here.

I can sum my whole life up in one sentence: *a prodigal son cannot return if there is no father to return to.*

So, I am leaving Hollywood, leaving America and heading to Germany. Sparkle has set me up as a cabaret performer; he says the Negro will be a hit in Germany. Perhaps one day I'll tell you all about that, but it is yet to happen. I have no illusions.

I mourn few things. I am not a callous man, I just don't feel the urge to regret. What's the point? But I take some responsibility for the death of young Smith. I could have saved him if I'd given him that knowledge that had come to me in my hard scrabble years: All your life you will be pursued, because you are a black boy, because you have followed a man who had long dried up of high religious principle. A preacher is supposed to give solace, and I gave none.

I will not look forward to calamity in the years to come. That is my new covenant with my Lord.

Yesterday a young woman who danced with me in a movie gave me the New Testament. I read it through that same night. This line troubles me:

A sower went out to sow his seed; and as he sowed, some fell on the path, and was trampled on, and they fell among the thorns, and the thorns grew with it and choked it. Some fell into good soil and grew, and when it grew it produced a hundredfold.

170

Such hope as compared to the Old Testament, which I still love above all things. Yes, I still have Mama's Bible. It is still marked at this passage: *Thinkest thou this to be right, that thou saidst, My righteousness is more than God's?*

But then, I will always remember what W.E. B. DuBois wrote about John: ...*a new dignity crept into his walk.*

THE END

Discussion Group Questions for *Elijah Rising* (Book I in the Elijah Trilogy)

The following discussion questions are intended to help you and your reading group analyze interesting themes and the dynamics of the characters in Lyn LeJeune's *Elijah Rising*.

1. The story takes place between the years 1917 and 1925. What similarities do you see between the cultural landscape then and now, especially in matters of race, sexuality, religion and politics?
2. The work is infused with the physical longing between the two main characters, Michael and Elijah. Does it seem as though Michael is able to love all of Elijah, yet Elijah can only love parts of Michael? Or is it the other way around? Why are they drawn to each other when it seems, at the onset, they come from such different worlds? What are their ideas of what it is to love another person? Did they each fear the times in which they lived or themselves?
3. Why does Michael think so little of his own worth, while Elijah thinks he can bring redemption to the world? What is the concept of redemption in Michael and Elijah's view? How about yours?
4. Does Michael see the world in realistic terms? Does Elijah?
5. If you were traveling with Elijah into the "soul of America" what would you think about the purpose of your journey?
6. What are some of the similarities between the two main characters' relationship with their mothers? Differences? How do these relationships shape them?
7. What about their fathers?
8. Why did the author make the main characters black and white and male?
9. What is the significance of war and music to the dramatic themes of *Elijah Rising*?
10. Are there "two Americas" in *Elijah Rising*? One, New York and the east, the other, the southwestern U.S. What about Hollywood?
11. On the first page of the book, Michael makes this statement when he sees a photograph of Elijah in the newspaper: "Little Washington, now the great Elijah, has made his way to a home, a place to belong, and planted himself in America." Where is Michael's home?

174

12. Not until the end of the book does Elijah read *The New Testament*. Why did the author place *The Old Testament* in Elijah's hands? And why did the author choose this passage from *The New Testament* at the end of the first book of *The Elijah Trilogy*?

A sower went out to sow his seed; and as he sowed, some fell on the path, and was trampled on, and they fell among the thorns, and the thorns grew with it and choked it. Some fell into good soil and grew, and when it grew it produced a hundredfold.

13. Why did the author write the last chapter in Elijah's voice rather than Michael's?

14. What is the symbolism of Young Smith's death?

15. What is the significance of Blind Willie Johnson to the story?

16. Who is Zelda? What does she do for Michael in terms of his accepting his sexuality?

17. How did Michael and Elijah change throughout the book? What did they discover about themselves, the world, and each other?

18. What is the meaning of the following statement, made by Michael, to the main theme of the story? "How extraordinary that they would allow his preaching, this black man, in this age of fury."

19. Often, when reading a book about dynamic and changing characters, we are haunted by their lives and wonder what will become of them. Do you think that Michael and Elijah will survive and be happy?

20. Some of the characters we do not hear from directly (in their own voice)—for example, Billy Sunday, the head of the KKK, William Jennings Bryan, Sparkle, John Reed, Mama Jones – who would you have liked to hear most from and why?

Discover more great titles from inGroup Press:

The Literary Party: Growing Up Gay and Amish in America by James Schwartz (ISBN-13: 978-1935725053)

What comes to mind when you think about the Amish? For most people, the popular imagery is a horse and buggy, farmhouses with no electricity, funny hats, and bowl haircuts. Ever since Weird Al Yankovich recorded "Amish Paradise", certain stereotypes have persisted in popular culture. None of these stereotypes, however, have included *gay*.

The Literary Party: Growing Up Gay and Amish in America is one of those books that shatter stereotypes. Written by James Schwartz, a Michigan native who grew up in an Old Order Amish community, *The Literary Party* offers an eye-opening portrait of gay life within a religious group known for its privacy and secrecy. When the documentary *Devil's Playground* (2002) examined rumspringa—a period when Amish teenagers can engage in rebellious behavior before choosing whether or not to remain in the church—viewers were shocked. Watching an Amish teen ride a horse and buggy to a party where drinking and smoking were involved shattered popular myths. Schwartz's *Literary Party* continues that theme. From juvenile flirtations to gay clubs, drag, love, and sex, Schwartz tells his story through poetry that is moving, heartfelt, political, and celebratory.

Finally Out: Letting Go of Living Straight, A Psychiatrist's Own Story by Loren A. Olson, M.D. (ISBN-13: 978-1935725039)

Average ... he's not. Not only did Olson complete medical school, serve four years as a flight surgeon in the U.S. Navy, and embark upon a successful career as a psychiatrist; he also had a compatible eighteen year marriage and raised two daughters with his attorney wife, Lynn, before facing up to a difficult truth about himself: he is gay.

There are approximately 7 million adult gay and bisexual men in the United States. Although there are still hurdles to overcome regarding gay acceptance, for many young men today their sexual orientation is an accepted part of their identity. But in decades past, when Olson was growing up in the Midwest in the 1950's, it was a "sin" to be homosexual. The most dreaded names a boy could be called were "sissy," "fairy," and "queer."

Olson had a vague awareness that he was different from other boys. As he matured he attributed his sexual ambivalence to his dad's death when he was three; he was confused about his manhood, he reasoned, because he lacked a male role model. Then came medical school, the navy, his psychiatric residency, marriage and raising a family. While meaningful and satisfying life choices, they served to protect him from his intensifying feelings of attraction towards men. If on occasion Olson questioned whether he might be bisexual, he pushed the thought from his consciousness. He was a "heterosexual, with a little quirk" he decided.

But at 40, after decades of inner conflict, Olson was drawn to an affair with a married man. Although short-lived, it was the defining moment. Not long after the relationship ended, he made a heart wrenching decision: he sought a divorce and began the complicated journey of "coming out" – to his wife, kids, mother, colleagues and friends. Facing down fears that the news would shatter his family and ruin his career, a lifetime of struggle began to resolve itself. Olson summoned the integrity to figure out who he really was and what it would mean to live as that person.

With professional insight Olson examines his personal transformation from a "straight" man living in a heterosexual world to a gay man beginning his education anew. He punctuates his story with revealing statistics from his interviews with gay men around the world and established studies on homo- sexuality, and with surprising historical facts that provide perspective on global cultural norms.

Part personal memoir and part psychological treatise, "Finally Out" offers a rigorous look at why some gay men live straight lives and never come to terms with their true sexual orientation; why some men believe they are "too straight to be gay" even while engaging in secret sex with other men – and the challenges faced by those who choose to "come out" after living half a lifetime or more closeted.

inGroupPress.com

Made in the USA
Charleston, SC
30 September 2011